AMÉLIE NOTHOMB

The Book of Proper Names

Translated from the French
by Shaun Whiteside

faber and faber

First published in 2002
by Albin Michel, France

First published in the UK in 2004
by Faber and Faber Limited
3 Queen Square London WCIN 3AU
This paperback edition published in 2005

Typeset by Faber and Faber Limited
Printed in England by Mackays of Chatham plc, Chatham, Kent

A CIP record for this book
is available from the British Library

ISBN 0-571-22344-3

2 4 6 8 10 9 7 5 3 1

THE BOOK OF PROPER NAMES

LUCETTE WAS IN HER EIGHTH HOUR of insomnia. The baby in her womb had been hiccuping since the previous day. Every four or five seconds a gigantic jolt shook the body of the little nineteen-year-old girl who had decided to become a wife and mother a year before.

The fairy tale had begun like a dream: Fabien was handsome, he declared himself willing to do anything for her, and she had taken him at his word. The idea of playing at marriage had amused the boy, who was the same age as herself, and her family, puzzled and touched, had watched the two children putting on their wedding clothes.

Shortly afterwards, triumphantly, Lucette had announced that she was pregnant.

Her big sister had asked her: 'Isn't it a bit soon?'

'It'll never be soon enough!' the girl had replied delightedly.

Little by little the fairy tale had soured. Fabien and Lucette argued a lot. Where once he had been so happy about her pregnancy, he now said, 'You might consider not going crazy when the kid's around!'

'Are you threatening me?'

Off he went, slamming the door.

But she was sure she wasn't crazy. She wanted life to be strong and dense. Wouldn't you have had to be crazy to want anything else? She wanted every day, every year, to bring her the absolute maximum.

Now, she could see that Fabien wasn't a match for her. He was an ordinary boy. He had played at getting married, and now he was playing at being a married man. There was nothing of the Prince Charming about him. He repelled her. He said, 'There she goes, throwing a tantrum.'

Sometimes he was nice. He would stroke her belly, saying, 'If it's a boy, it'll be Tanguy. If it's a girl, it'll be Joëlle.'

Lucette thought to herself that she hated those names.

In her grandfather's library she had picked up an encyclopaedia from the previous century. It contained phantasmagorical first names that promised great destinies. Lucette conscientiously jotted them down on bits of paper that she sometimes lost. Later people would find scattered around the place scraps of paper bearing the word 'Eleuthère' or 'Lutegarde', and no one could guess the meaning of these cryptic and surreal messages.

The baby had started to move very early. The gynaecologist said he had never before encountered such an active foetus.

'It's unbelievable!'

Lucette smiled. Her child was exceptional already. It was in those recent times when it was not yet possible to know the child's sex in advance. The pregnant girl didn't care.

'Whichever sex it is, it's going to be a dancer,' she had decreed, her head full of dreams.

'No,' said Fabien, 'it's going to be a footballer or a pain in the arse.'

She looked daggers at him. He meant nothing by it, it was just a tease. But in such childish observations, she saw the mark of insurmountable vulgarity.

When she was on her own and the foetus moved like a mad thing, she would speak tenderly to it: 'Go on, dance, my baby. I'll protect you, I won't let you be a footballing Tanguy or a pain-in-the-arse Joëlle; you'll be free to dance wherever you like: at the Paris Opéra, or for little groups of bohemians.'

Little by little, Fabien had taken to disappearing for whole afternoons. He left after lunch, and came back at about ten o'clock in the evening, without a word of explanation. Exhausted by her pregnancy, Lucette hadn't the strength to wait for him. She was already asleep by the time he came back. In the morning he stayed in bed until half past eleven. He had a bowl of coffee with a cigarette, which he smoked as he stared into the void.

'Are you all right? Not tiring yourself?' she asked him one day.

'What about you?' he replied.

'I'm having a baby. You aware of that?'

'And how. It's the only thing you ever talk about.'

'Well, I can assure you it's very tiring, being pregnant.'

'That's not my fault. You're the one who wanted it. I can't carry the thing for you.'

'Any chance of knowing what you get up to in the afternoon?'

'No.'

She exploded with rage. 'I don't know anything any more! You tell me nothing!'

'You're not interested in anything apart from the baby.'

'All you have to do is be interesting. Then I'll be interested in you.'

'I *am* interesting.'

'Go on, then, interest me, let's see if you're up to it!'

He sighed and went off to get a box. Out of it he took a handgun. She opened her eyes wide.

'That's what I do in the afternoon. I shoot.'

'Where do you do that?'

'A secret club. It doesn't matter.'

'Are there real bullets in there?'

'Yes.'

'For killing people?'

'Amongst other things.'

She stroked the gun, fascinated.

'I'm getting good, you know. I get the bullseye first time. You can't imagine the feeling. I love it. Once I get started, I can't stop.'

'I understand that.'

They didn't understand each other often.

Lucette's big sister, who had two small children, came to see her. Her sister adored her. She thought Lucette was so pretty, so frail and with that enormous belly. One day they had an argument.

'You should tell him to go and get a job. He's going to be a father.'

'We're nineteen. Our parents pay for everything.'

'They won't go on paying for ever.'

'Why are you bothering me with all this nonsense?'

'It is important, you know.'

'You always have to come and ruin my happiness!'

'What are you on about?'

'And now you're going to tell me I have to be sensible, and blah blah blah!'

'You're off your head! I haven't said anything of the sort!'

'That's it! I'm off my head! That's what I was waiting for you to say! You're jealous of me! You want to destroy me!'

'Come on, Lucette . . .'

'Get out,' she screamed.

Her big sister left, aghast. She had always known that her baby sister was fragile, but things were assuming worrying proportions.

From then on, when her sister rang her up, Lucette put the phone down the moment she heard her voice.

'I've got enough problems like that,' she thought to herself.

In fact, without admitting it, she felt that she was up against the wall, and her big sister knew that. How would they ever earn a livelihood? Fabien wasn't interested in anything apart from guns, and she was completely hopeless. None the less, she wasn't going to be a supermarket cashier. And besides, she wasn't sure she was up to it.

She put a pillow over her head to stop thinking about it.

So that night the baby had hiccups in Lucette's belly.

You can't imagine the impact a hiccuping foetus has on a little pregnant girl when her nerves are on edge.

As to Fabien, he was blissfully asleep. She was in her eighth hour of insomnia, and her eighth month of pregnancy. Her vast belly made her feel as though she held a time bomb inside her.

Each hiccup seemed to her to match the tick-tock-tick that was bringing the moment of the explosion ever closer. Her fantasy became a reality: there was a real conflagration going on in Lucette's head.

She got to her feet, driven by a sudden conviction that made her open her eyes wide.

She went to get the revolver from where Fabien had hidden it. She came back towards the bed where the boy was sleeping. She looked at his handsome face as she aimed at his temple and murmured, 'I do love you, but I've got to protect the baby.'

She put the barrel to his head and fired until the magazine was empty.

She looked at the blood on the wall. Then, very calmly, she called the police. 'I've just killed my husband. You'd better come.'

WHEN THE POLICE ARRIVED, they were welcomed by a child, heavily pregnant, holding a handgun in her right hand.

'Put down the weapon!' they said threateningly.

'It's not loaded now,' she replied, obeying.

She led the policemen over to the marriage bed to show them her work.

'Should we take her to the station, or to the hospital?'

'Why the hospital? There's nothing wrong with me.'

'We don't know that. But you are pregnant.'

'I'm not about to give birth. Take me to the police station,' she demanded, as though it were her right.

When it was over, she was told that she could call a lawyer. She said there was no need. A man in an office asked her endless questions, including:

'Why did you kill your husband?'

'The baby in my belly had hiccups.'

'And?'

'Nothing. I killed Fabien.'

'You killed him because the baby had hiccups?'

She looked taken aback, before answering, 'No. It's not as simple as that. And anyway, the baby doesn't have hiccups any more.'

'You killed your husband to get rid of your baby's hiccups?'

She laughed, inappropriately. 'No, that would be absurd.'

'Why did you kill your husband?'

'To protect my baby,' she affirmed, this time wearing a tragic expression.

'I see. Your husband had threatened the baby?'

'Yes.'

'You should have said so straight away.'

'Yes.'

'And what did he threaten it with?'

'He wanted to call it Tanguy if it was a boy and Joëlle if it was a girl.'

'What else?'

'That's it.'

'You killed your husband because you didn't like his choice of names?'

She frowned. She felt her argument lacked a certain something, and yet she was sure she was right. She understood very clearly what she had done, and found it all the more frustrating that she couldn't explain it. So she decided to say nothing.

'Are you sure you don't want a lawyer?'

She was sure. How could she have explained it to a lawyer? He would have thought she was a lunatic, like everyone else. The more she spoke, the more people thought she was a lunatic. In that case, she'd keep her trap shut.

She was put in a cell. A nurse came to see her every day.

When she was told that her mother or her big sister had come to visit, she refused to see them.

She only answered questions about her pregnancy. Apart from that, she stayed mute.

In her head, she talked to herself: 'I was right to kill Fabien. He wasn't bad, he was mediocre. The only thing about him that wasn't mediocre was his handgun, but he would only have used it in a mediocre way, against the little local thugs, or else he'd have let the baby play with it. I was right to turn it on him. Wanting to call your child Tanguy or Joëlle is the same as wanting to give them a mediocre world, a closed horizon. As for me, I want my baby to have infinity within reach. I want my child not to feel limited by anything at all, I want my baby's first name to suggest an uncommon destiny.'

In prison, Lucette gave birth to a little girl. She took her in her arms and looked at her with all the love in the world. No one had ever seen a more delighted young mother.

'You're too beautiful!' she told the baby, over and over again.

'What are you going to call her?'

'Plectrude.'

A delegation of warders, psychologists, vague-looking

lawyers and even vaguer-looking doctors crowded around Lucette to protest: she couldn't give her daughter a name like that.

'Yes I can. There was a Saint Plectrude. I can't remember what she did, but she did exist.'

A specialist was consulted; he confirmed this as the truth.

'Think of the child, Lucette.'

'That's all I am thinking about.'

'It'll only cause her problems.'

'It will tell people that she's exceptional.'

'You can be called Marie and be exceptional.'

'Marie doesn't protect you. Plectrude protects you: that "rude" at the end sounds like a shield.'

'So call her Gertrude, then. It's easier to deal with.'

'No. The first part of "Plectrude" sounds like a pectoral: the name is a talisman.'

'The name is grotesque and your child will be a laughing stock.'

'No: it will make her strong enough to defend herself.'

'Why give her any sort of reason to defend herself? She's going to have enough problems to deal with anyway!'

'Are you referring to me?'

'Among other things.'

'Don't worry, I don't intend to trouble her for long. And now, listen to me: I'm in prison, I'm deprived of my rights. The only freedom I have left is to name my child as I wish to.'

'That's selfish, Lucette.'

'Quite the reverse. And anyway, it has nothing to do with you.'

She had the baby baptized in prison so that she could be sure of controlling everything.

That very night she made a rope from some torn sheets and hanged herself in her cell. In the morning, they found her weightless corpse. She hadn't left a letter or an explanation. Her daughter's first name, on which she had insisted so much, took the place of a will.

CLÉMENCE, LUCETTE'S OLDER SISTER, came to the prison to get the baby. The authorities were only too happy to get rid of the child, born as it was in such horribly inauspicious circumstances.

Clémence and her husband Denis had two children of four and two, Nicole and Béatrice. They decided that Plectrude would be their third.

Nicole and Béatrice came to look at their new sister. They had no reason to think that she was Lucette's daughter. And anyway, they had barely been aware of Lucette's existence.

They were too little to realize that her name was something of a mouthful, and adopted her, despite having some problems with the pronunciation. For a long time they called her 'Plecrude'.

Never had anyone seen a baby more skilled at drawing love to her. Was she aware that she had been born in tragic circumstances? With heart-rending glances she begged those around her to disregard the fact. It should be added that she had a trump card in this respect: improbably beautiful eyes.

The newborn baby, small and thin, fixed her target with her vast gaze – vast in both size and meaning. Her huge, magnificent eyes told Clémence and Denis: 'Love me! Your destiny is to love me! I'm only eight weeks old, but I'm still a magnificent creature! If you knew, if you only knew . . .'

Denis and Clémence seemed to know. From the very first, they felt a kind of admiration for Plectrude. Everything about her was strange, from the unbearable slowness with which she drank from her bottle to the way she never cried, the fact that she slept little at night and a great deal during the day, and the way she pointed with a resolute finger at things she craved.

She looked seriously, profoundly, at anyone who picked her up, as though to say that this was the beginning of a great love story, and that they had every reason to be stirred to the quick.

Clémence, who had loved her late sister to distraction, transferred her passion to Plectrude. She didn't love her any more than she did her own two children: she loved her in a different way. Nicole and Béatrice inspired an overwhelming tenderness in her; Plectrude inspired her veneration.

Her two elder daughters were pretty, sweet, intelligent, agreeable; the little last one was extraordinary – splendid, intense, enigmatic, crazy.

Denis too was wild about her from the first, and he remained so. But nothing could match the sacred love that Clémence devoted to her. There was a wild passion between Lucette's sister and her daughter.

Plectrude had no appetite, and she grew as slowly as she ate. It was desperate. Nicole and Béatrice devoured and grew before your very eyes. They had round, pink cheeks that delighted their parents. As for Plectrude, all that grew was her eyes.

'Are we really going to call her that?' Denis asked one day.

'Of course. My sister insisted on the name.'

'Your sister was mad.'

'No. My sister was fragile. Anyway, I think Plectrude's pretty.'

'Really?'

'Yes. And it suits her.'

'I don't agree. She looks like a fairy. I'd have called her Aurore.'

'It's too late. The girls have already adopted her under her real name. And I assure you that it does suit her: it's like the name of a gothic princess.'

'Poor kid! Things are going to be hard at school.'

'Not for her. She has enough personality to cope.'

Plectrude uttered her first word at a normal age, and it was 'Mama!'

Clémence went into ecstasies. Laughing, Denis pointed out that the first word of all her children – and all the children in the world – was 'mama'.

'This is different,' said Clémence.

For a very long time, 'mama' was Plectrude's only word.

Like the umbilical cord, this word was sufficient connection with the world. From the first, she had enunciated the word perfectly, in a confident voice and with a clear 'ah' sound at the end, unlike the 'mamamamam' of most babies.

She uttered the word rarely but when she did, it was with a solemn clarity that commanded attention. You would have sworn that she chose her moments for maximum effect.

Clémence had been six when Lucette was born: she remembered very clearly what her sister had been like at birth, at the age of one, at two and so on. No confusion was possible:

'Lucette was ordinary. She cried a lot, she was adorable and unbearable by turns. There was nothing exceptional about her. Plectrude is nothing like her: she's silent, serious, thoughtful. You can sense how intelligent she is.'

Denis gently mocked his wife: 'Stop talking about her as though she were the second coming. She's a charming child, that's all.'

He lifted her up above his head, his heart melting.

Much later, Plectrude said, 'Papa.'

The next day, out of pure diplomacy, she said, 'Nicole' and 'Béatrice'.

Her elocution was impeccable.

She started speaking as parsimoniously as she ate. Each new word demanded as much concentration and meditation as the new types of food that appeared on her plate.

Whenever she saw an unfamiliar vegetable in the depths of her mashed potato, she pointed it out to Clémence.

'That?' she asked.

'That's leek. Leek. You try it, it's very good.'

Plectrude first of all spent half an hour contemplating the piece of leek in her spoon. She brought it up to her nose to gauge its scent, then she went on studying it for ages and ages.

'It's cold now!' said Denis crossly.

She didn't care. When she estimated that it was time to bring her examination to an end, she took the food in her mouth and tasted it for ages. She delivered no verdict: she began the experiment over again with a second piece, then a third. The most astonishing thing was that she proceeded in this fashion even when her final judgement, after four attempts, was: 'I hate it.'

Normally, when a child hates some food, she knows she does as soon as she has touched it with her tongue. Plectrude, on the other hand, wanted to be sure of her tastes.

It was the same with words; she stored any verbal novelties inside her and examined them from every angle before taking them out again, most often out of context, to everyone's surprise: 'Giraffe!'

Why did she say 'giraffe' when they were preparing to go for a walk? She was suspected of not understanding her own declarations. And yet she did understand. It was just that her thoughts were independent of any external contingencies. All of a sudden, just as she was slipping on her coat, Plectrude's mind had finished digesting the enormity of the neck and feet of the giraffe: so she had to utter its name, to alert people to the emergence of the giraffe into her internal universe.

'Have you noticed how lovely her voice is?' said Clémence.

'Have you ever heard a child who didn't have a pretty voice?' observed Denis.

'Exactly! Her voice isn't pretty, it's lovely,' she replied.

In September she was sent to nursery school.

'She'll be three in a month. It might be a bit soon.'

That wasn't the problem.

After a few days, the teacher told Clémence that she couldn't keep Plectrude.

'She's still very young, isn't she?'

'No, that's not it. I've got younger children than her in the class.'

'So?'

'It's because of her eyes.'

'What?'

'She makes the other children cry just by staring at them. And I have to say that I understand them. *I* feel uneasy when she stares at me.'

Clémence, filled with pride, announced to everyone that her daughter had been expelled from nursery school because of her eyes. No one had ever heard anything like it.

PEOPLE WERE ALREADY MURMURING, 'Have you ever heard of a child being expelled from nursery school?'

'And because of their eyes, at that!'

'It's true that the kid does have a funny way of staring at you!'

'The two older ones are so well behaved, so nice. That last one's a little demon!'

Did people know the circumstances of her birth, or didn't they? Clémence was careful not to question her neighbours on the matter. She preferred to think that Plectrude's descent from her was taken for granted.

She was delighted that she was remaining so close to the child. Every morning Denis set off for work, driving the two older children, one to school and the other to nursery. Clémence stayed alone with the last little girl.

As soon as the door closed on her husband and children, she transformed into another person. She became the composite of fairy and witch that the mere presence of Plectrude awoke within her.

'The coast is clear. Let's go and change.'

She changed in the most profound sense of that word; not only did she take off her normal clothes to wrap herself up in the luxurious fabrics that made her look like an Indian queen, but she swapped her maternal soul for that of a phantasmagorical creature blessed with exceptional powers.

Under the child's steady gaze, the twenty-eight-year-old liberated from within her breast the sixteen-year-old fairy and the ten-thousand-year-old witch that dwelt there.

Then she undressed the child and clothed her again in the princess's dress that she had secretly bought for her. She took her by the hand and led her in front of the big mirror, where they contemplated themselves.

'Have you seen how beautiful we are?'

Plectrude sighed with happiness.

Then Clémence would dance, to charm her little three-year-old. Plectrude joined in delightedly. Clémence held her hands, then suddenly grabbed Plectrude by the waist and made her fly through the air.

Plectrude uttered cries of joy.

'Now let's look at the things,' demanded the child, who knew this ritual.

'What things?' asked Clémence, pretending not to know.

'The princess things.'

The princess things were the objects which, for one reason or another, had been selected as noble, magnificent, unusual or rare – worthy, in fact, of the admiration of such an august person as the little girl.

On the oriental carpet in the drawing room Clémence gathered together her old jewels, carmine velvet slippers that she had worn for only a single evening, a little lorgnette, its lenses set in Art Nouveau gold, the silver cigarette-box, the brass Arab flask incrusted with impressive-looking fake stones, a pair of white lace gloves, the gaudy plastic medieval rings from a coin-operated toy distributor, and the gold cardboard crown from the procession of the Three Kings.

So they had before them a pile of the most disparate objects that they both found marvellous: if you half-closed your eyes, you would have said it was a real treasure-trove.

Mouth agape, the little girl stared at this pirate's booty. She picked up each object in turn and studied it with ecstatic gravity.

Sometimes Clémence dressed her up in all the jewels and the slippers; then she handed her the lorgnette and said, 'Now you can see how beautiful you are.'

Holding her breath, the little girl looked at her reflection in the mirror: staring through the gilded circles she discovered a three-year-old queen, a brightly coloured priestess, a Persian bride on her wedding day, a Byzantine saint posing for an ikon. In this crazed image she recognized herself.

Anyone might have burst out laughing at the sight of this tiny child, got up like some insane reliquary. Clémence smiled but didn't laugh: what struck her, more than the comedy of the scene, was the beauty of the little girl. She was as beautiful as the engravings found in fairy-tale collections from a long time ago.

'Children these days aren't as beautiful as that,' she thought absurdly – the children of the past were surely no better.

Often she put on some 'princess music' (Tchaikovsky, Prokofiev) and prepared a child's snack in the guise of lunch: gingerbread, chocolate cakes, apple turnovers, amaretti biscuits, vanilla flan, and, to drink, sweet cider and almond syrup.

Clémence would spread these treats out on the table with a mixture of shame and amusement: she would never have allowed her two older daughters to eat only sweets. She justified herself by reflecting that Plectrude was different: 'It's a meal for fairy-tale children.'

She closed the curtains, lit candles and called the little girl in. Plectrude barely nibbled, listening with big, attentive eyes to what her mother told her.

At about two o'clock in the afternoon, Clémence habitually realized with a start that the older girls would be finishing school in barely three hours, and that she had carried out none of the tasks that a mother has to perform.

She would change hastily into her ordinary clothes, run to the corner shop to buy proper food, come back to get the flat looking halfway decent, throw the dirty laundry into the washing machine and then set off for the school and the nursery to get the children. In her haste, she rarely had the time or the presence of mind to remove Plectrude's disguise – for the simple reason that in her eyes it wasn't a disguise.

So what people saw was a cheerful young woman walking along the street, holding by the hand a microscopic creature wearing clothes more extravagant than anything the princesses in the *Thousand and One Nights* would have dared to put on.

At the end of school, this spectacle provoked in turn perplexity, laughter, amazement and disapproval.

Nicole and Béatrice always uttered cries of joy when they saw their little sister's clothes, but some mothers said in strident voices:

'No child should be dressed up like that!'

'She isn't a circus animal.'

'I wouldn't be surprised if that girl turned out badly later on.'

'It's unspeakable, using children to draw attention to yourself like that.'

There were also adults less stupid than these, whose hearts melted at the sight of the apparition. The apparition herself took pleasure from this, thinking it quite normal to be looked at in that way, for she had noticed, in the mirror, that she was very beautiful – and had felt a voluptuous excitement in consequence.

Here we should open a parenthesis in order to conclude an idle beginning that has already gone on too long. This might be called the Arsinoé encyclical.

In Molière's *The Misanthrope*, the young, pretty and flirtatious Célimène finds herself being scolded by the old and bitter Arsinoé who, green with jealousy, comes to tell her that she should not enjoy her beauty so much. Célimène gives her an utterly delectable reply. Alas, Molière's genius will have counted for nothing, since almost four centuries later, people persist in delivering dry, moralistic, wet-blanket obloquies when anyone has the misfortune to smile at her own reflection.

The author of these lines has never felt any pleasure at seeing herself in a mirror, but had such grace been bestowed upon her, she would not have refused herself that innocent pleasure.

This discourse is addressed particularly to all the Arsinoés in the world: in fact, what more is there to say on the subject? Who are these fortunate creatures harming by enjoying their own beauty? Are they not rather the benefactors of our sad condition, by allowing us to gaze upon such marvellous faces?

Here the author is not talking about those who have turned fake prettiness into a principle of contempt and exclusiveness, but those who, simply delighted by their own image, wish to bind others to their own natural joy.

If these Arsinoés used the same energy to try and get the best out of their own physiques that they devote to ranting at girls like Célimène, they would be only half as ugly as they are.

By the end of school, Arsinoés of all ages were furious with Plectrude. Good Célimène that she was, she didn't care, and paid attention only to her admirers, on whose faces she saw enchantment and surprise. She took an innocent pleasure in that, which made her even more beautiful.

Clémence would return with the three children to the flat. As the older girls got on with their homework or did a little drawing, she prepared proper meals – ham, mashed potato – sometimes smiling at the different kinds of food she gave her various offspring.

But she could not have been accused of favouritism: she loved all her three children equally. Each one had a love in the image of the one who inspired it: well-behaved and solid for Nicole and Béatrice, wild and enchanted for Plectrude. She was no less good a mother for that.

When the little one was asked what she would like for her fourth birthday, she replied without a moment's hesitation: 'Ballet shoes.'

A subtle way of telling her parents what she wanted to be when she grew up. Nothing would have given Clémence greater pleasure: at the age of fifteen she had failed the entrance exam for the 'petits rats' of the Paris Opéra, and had never got over it.

Plectrude was signed up for a course of ballet lessons for four-year-old beginners. Not only was she not expelled because of her intense gaze, it was immediately seen as a sign of distinction.

'This little girl has the eyes of a dancer,' said the teacher.

'How can anyone have the eyes of a dancer?' asked Clémence, astonished. 'Wouldn't you say that she has a dancer's body, a dancer's grace?'

'Yes, she has all that. But she also has a dancer's eyes, and, believe me, it's the most important and the rarest thing. If a ballerina has no gaze, she will never dance to the full.'

What was certain was that Plectrude's eyes attained, when she danced, an extraordinary intensity. 'She's found herself,' thought Clémence.

BY THE AGE OF FIVE, THE LITTLE GIRL was still not going to nursery school. Her mother guessed that going to ballet classes four times a week was enough to teach her the art of living with other children.

'They teach other things in nursery school,' Denis protested.

'Does she really need to know how to stick stickers, and make pasta necklaces and macramé?' said his wife, staring at the ceiling.

In fact, Clémence wanted to prolong her intimacy with the little girl for as long as she possibly could. She adored the days she spent in her company. And the dance lessons had one undeniable superiority over nursery school: the mother was allowed to be present.

She watched the child twirling, ecstatic with pride: 'The girl has talent!' In comparison, the other little girls looked like ducklings.

After classes, the teacher made a point of coming to tell her, 'She's got to stay at it. She's quite exceptional.'

Clémence brought her daughter back to the flat, repeating the compliments she had received about her. Plectrude accepted them with the grace of a diva.

'Anyway, nursery school isn't compulsory,' Denis concluded with a certain amused fatalism, typical of the submissive husband.

But – alas! – infants' school was compulsory.

In August, as her husband was preparing to put Plectrude's name down for it, her mother protested: 'She's only five years old!'

'She'll be six in October.'

This time he kept to his word. And on the first of September it was not two, but three children that were driven to school.

Besides, the last of Clémence's daughters was not opposed to the idea. She was rather boastful about trying on her satchel. So there were strange scenes as Plectrude set off for her new school: this time it was the mother who wept as she saw the child leaving.

Plectrude was soon disenchanted. It was very different from ballet lessons. You had to stay sitting down for hours without moving. You had to listen to a woman who wasn't saying anything interesting.

Break time came. She dashed into the playground to practise her *jetés*. Her poor legs had been motionless for far too long.

As she did this the other children played together: most of them had known each other since nursery school. They told each other things. Plectrude wondered what on earth they could have to tell each other.

She went closer to listen. It was an uninterrupted murmur, produced by a large number of voices, not all of which she could match to their owners: they were talking about the teacher, holidays, someone called Magali, playing elastics, and give me a chocolate bar, and Magali's my friend, shut up you're too stupid, aaaaaooww, haven't you got any Snickers, why am I not in Magali's class, stop it, we're not going to play with you, I'm going to tell teacher, ooh you sneak, all you had to do was stop pushing me, Magali likes me more than you, and anyway your shoes are horrible, *stop* it, girls are so stupid, I'm glad I'm not in your class, and Magali . . .

Plectrude ran off, terrified.

And then you had to listen to the teacher again. What she said wasn't always interesting: at least it was more homogeneous than the children's chatter. It would have been bearable if there hadn't been that duty of staying immobile. Fortunately there was a window.

'Hey, you!'

At the fifth 'Hey, you!', and by virtue of the fact that the whole class was laughing, Plectrude worked out that she was the one being addressed, and turned towards everyone with startled eyes.

'You're a slow one!' said the teacher.

All the children had turned round to look at the girl who had been singled out. It was an awful feeling. The little dancer wondered what her crime could possibly be.

'You look at me, not the window!' the woman concluded.

As there was no possible answer to this, the child said nothing.

'You say, "Yes, miss"!'

'Yes, miss.'

'What's your name?' the teacher asked, as though she was thinking, 'I've got my eye on you!'

'Plectrude.'

'I'm sorry?'

'Plectrude,' she articulated in a clear voice.

The children were still too young to be aware of the outrageousness of the name. The teacher opened her eyes wide, checked on her register, and finally said, 'Well, if you're trying to show off, you've succeeded.'

As though she had chosen her own first name.

The girl thought, 'She's one to talk! She's the one who's been showing off all morning! You can tell – she can't bear not to be looked at. She wants to get herself noticed, but she's not in the slightest bit interesting!'

But because the teacher was the boss, the child obeyed. She started staring at her with her eyes wide open. Miss was knocked off balance, but didn't dare protest, for fear of giving contradictory instructions.

The worst thing happened at lunchtime. The pupils were led into a vast canteen dominated by a characteristic smell, a mixture of children's vomit and disinfectant.

They had to sit down at tables of ten. Plectrude didn't know where to go and closed her eyes so as not to be chosen. A deluge led her to a table full of strangers.

Some ladies brought in dishes that were unidentifiable both in content and in colour. Panicking, Plectrude could not bring herself to put foreign bodies on to her plate. So the ladies served her themselves, and she found herself looking at a dish full of greenish mush and little squares of brown meat.

She wondered what she had done to deserve such a cruel fate. Until then, as far as she was concerned, lunch had been a pure enchantment: by candlelight, protected from the world by red velvet hangings, a beautiful mother, magnificently dressed, brought her cakes and creams that she wasn't even forced to eat, to the sound of heavenly music. And here, amidst the cries of hideous, dirty children, in an ugly and funny-smelling hall, they chucked green mush into her plate and told her that she wasn't to leave the canteen before she'd choked down the lot.

Scandalized by the injustice of fate, the little one set about clearing her plate. It was terrifying. She had terrible trouble swallowing. Halfway through, she vomited into her plate and understood the source of the smell.

'Ugh, you're disgusting!' the children said to her.

A lady came to take her plate away and sighed, 'Oh, my goodness!'

At least she wasn't forced to eat anything else that day.

After this nightmare she had to listen, once again, to the woman who was trying, without success, to draw attention to herself. On the blackboard, she jotted down combinations of letters that weren't even nice to look at. At half past four, Plectrude was finally allowed to leave this place, as absurd as it was abject. At going-home time, she spotted her mother, and ran towards her as one runs towards a place of safety.

Clémence had only to look to know how much her child had suffered. She pressed her in her arms and murmured comforting words: 'Now, now, it's over, it's over.'

'Really?' said the little girl hopefully. 'I won't be going back?'

'Yes you will. It's compulsory. But you'll get used to it.'

And Plectrude, aghast, understood that we aren't put on this planet to enjoy ourselves.

She didn't get used to it. School was hell, and it remained so.

Fortunately, there were the ballet lessons. Where what her schoolteacher taught was useless and awful, what her dance teacher taught was indispensable and sublime.

This discrepancy began to create some problems. After a few months, most of the children in the class were able to decipher letters and draw their shapes. As to Plectrude, she seemed to have decided that such matters had nothing to do with her: when her time came, and the teacher showed her a letter written on the board, she pronounced a sound at random, always completely wrong, making her lack of interest a little too obvious.

The teacher finally demanded to see this dunce's parents. Denis was embarrassed: Nicole and Béatrice were good pupils, and had not accustomed him to this kind of humiliation. Clémence, although she would not have admitted it, felt an obscure sort of pride: clearly, this little rebel didn't do anything the way anyone else did.

'If it goes on like this, she's going to be held back a year to repeat reception class!' the teacher told them menacingly.

Plectrude's mother widened her eyes admiringly: she had never heard of a child having to repeat reception. It struck her as brilliant, daring, aristocratic in its insolence. What child would dare to repeat reception class? Where even the most mediocre pupils got through without too much difficulty, her daughter was already proudly asserting her difference – no, her exceptional nature.

That wasn't how Denis saw it: 'We'll sort this out!' he told the teacher. 'We'll take control of the situation!'

'Is there any chance of her not repeating a year?' asked Clémence, filled with a hope that the others misinterpreted.

'Certainly. If she can learn to read her letters before the end of the school year.'

Plectrude's mother concealed her disappointment. It had been too lovely to be true!

'She will read them,' said Denis. 'And yet it's strange. The child seems very bright.'

'That's entirely possible. The problem is that she isn't interested.'

'She isn't interested!' thought Clémence. 'She's amazing! She isn't interested! What a character! Where other kids swallow the lot without a murmur, my Plectrude has already worked out what's interesting and what isn't!'

❤

'I'm not interested in it, Dad.'

'Come on, learning to read *is* interesting!' Denis protested.

'Why?'

'So that you can read stories.'

'Come off it. The teacher sometimes reads us stories from our reading book. It's so annoying that I stop listening two minutes in.'

Clémence mentally applauded.

'Are you going to repeat reception class? Is that what you want?' said Denis furiously.

'I want to be a dancer.'

'Even to be a dancer, you've got to get through reception.'

Clémence suddenly realized that her husband was right. She reacted immediately. She went and got a gigantic nineteenth-century book from her bedroom.

She took the child on her knees and religiously flicked through the collection of fairy stories with her. She was careful not to read them to her, and only to show her the lovely illustrations.

It was a shock in the child's life: she had never been filled with such wonder as when she discovered those princesses who were too magnificent to touch the ground with their feet, those princesses locked up in their towers who talked to bluebirds that were really princes, or disguised themselves as slatterns only to reappear even more sublime than before, four pages later.

At that moment she knew, with the certainty that only little girls are capable of, that one day she would be one of those creatures who fill toads with longing, foil wicked witches, and leave princes in a state of stunned submission.

'Don't worry,' Clémence said to Denis. 'She'll be reading by the end of the week.'

The truth exceeded her prognosis: two days later, Plectrude's brain had turned to its own advantage the boring and pointless letters it didn't realize it had absorbed in class, and found a coherence between signs, sounds and meaning. Two days later, she was reading a hundred times better than the best pupils in her reception class. Which means that there is only one key to knowledge, and that is desire.

She had seen the book of fairy tales as an instruction manual to help her become one of the princesses in the illustrations. Because reading was necessary to her now, her intelligence had absorbed it.

'Why didn't you show her that book before?' Denis cried in delight.

'That collection is a treasure-trove. I didn't want to spoil it by showing it to her too soon. She had to be old enough to appreciate a work of art.'

So, two days later, the teacher was aware of the miracle: the little dunce who, unlike everyone else, had not been able to identify a single letter, was now reading like the top pupil in a class of ten-year-olds.

In two days, she had learned what a professional hadn't managed to teach her in five months. The teacher thought her parents must have a secret method, and phoned them up to find out. Denis, mad with pride, told her the truth:

'We didn't do anything at all. We just showed her a book that was so beautiful it made her want to read. That's what was missing.'

In his naïveté, Plectrude's father didn't realize that he was making a dreadful blunder.

The teacher, who had never much cared for Plectrude, now began to hate her. Not only did she consider this miracle to be a personal humiliation, but she also felt for the little girl the hatred that a mediocre mind feels for a superior one: 'Miss Madam needed a beautiful book! Look at this one! This one's beautiful enough for everyone else!'

Perplexed and furious, the teacher picked up the reading book that was under attack and reread it from cover to cover. It contained the story of the daily life of Thierry, a smiling little boy, and his big sister Micheline, who made him bread and jam for his afternoon snack and kept him out of scrapes, because she was sensible.

'But it's charming!' she exclaimed to herself as she finished reading. 'It's fresh, it's delightful. What else could the silly goose possibly need?'

What she needed was gold, myrrh and frankincense, purple and lilies, midnight-blue velvet scattered with stars, engravings by Gustave Doré, little girls with lovely serious eyes and unsmiling mouths, gloomily seductive wolves, evil forests – she needed all kinds of things, but not little Thierry and his big sister Micheline.

From now on the teacher never missed an opportunity to voice her hatred of Plectrude. Because she remained bottom of the class in sums, the teacher called her 'the desperate case'. One day when she proved unable to carry out even the simplest of additions, Miss invited her to return to her seat, saying, 'As for you, there's no point in you making an effort. You'll never be able to do it.'

The reception-class pupils were still at that follow-my-leader age at which the adult is always right, and dissent is unthinkable. So Plectrude was the object of universal contempt.

In her ballet classes, by the same logic, she was the queen. The teacher was ecstatic about her abilities and, without daring to say so (because it would not have been a very good educational policy as far as the other children were concerned), treated her as the best pupil she had ever had in her life. Consequently, the little girls worshipped Plectrude and jostled one another to dance next to her.

As a result she had two quite distinct lives. There was school life, where it was Plectrude versus the rest, and life in her ballet class, where she was the star.

She was clear-sighted enough to realize that the children in her dance class might well be the first to despise her if they were in reception class with her. For that reason, Plectrude was distant towards the girls who sought her friendship – and that attitude further intensified the passion of the little ballerinas.

AT THE END OF THE YEAR, she just scrapped through her reception class by making a sustained effort at mathematics. As a reward, her parents gave her a barre so that she could practise her exercises in front of the big mirror. She spent her holidays training. By the end of August she could hold her foot in her hand.

When she returned to school after the holidays there was a surprise waiting for her: the composition of the class was the same as it had been the previous year, one important exception apart. There was a new girl.

She was a stranger to everyone except Plectrude, because she was Roselyne from her ballet lessons. Struck dumb with happiness to be in her idol's class, she asked permission to sit next to Plectrude. Never before had anyone asked to sit there: so the request was granted.

As far as Roselyne was concerned, Plectrude represented the absolute ideal. She spent hours studying that inaccessible muse who had miraculously become her neighbour at school.

Plectrude wondered whether that worship would survive the discovery of her unpopularity in the classroom. One day, when the teacher was remarking upon her mathematical weakness, the children ventured some ill-mannered comments about their fellow pupil. Roselyne flew into a rage at their behaviour, and said to the girl they were mocking, 'Have you seen how they are treating you?'

The dunce, who was used to it, shrugged her shoulders. Roselyne only admired her all the more and finally said, 'I hate them!'

It was then that Plectrude knew she had a friend.

It changed her life.

How can one explain the special prestige that friendship enjoys in the eyes of children? They believe, albeit wrongly, that it is the duty of their parents, their brothers and sisters, to love them. It never occurs to them to recognize merit in something that is, as far as they are concerned, merely part of the job. It is typical of children to say, 'I love them because they are my brother (my father, my sister . . .). It's compulsory.'

The friend, where a child is concerned, is the one who does the choosing. To have a friend is a privilege, not something to be expected by right. For a child, friendship is the supreme luxury – and luxury is what well-born souls need most ardently. Friendship brings with it a sense of the splendour of existence.

Returning to the flat, Plectrude solemnly announced: 'I've got a friend.'

It was the first time she had ever been heard to say that. Immediately Clémence felt a twinge in her heart. She very quickly managed to reason: there would never be any competition between the intruder and herself. Friends move on. Mothers don't.

'Invite her to dinner,' she said to her daughter.

Plectrude opened her eyes wide with terror.

'Why?'

'What do you mean, why? To introduce her to us. We want to meet your friend.'

It was on this occasion that the little girl discovered that when you wanted to meet someone, you invited them to dinner. It struck her as worrying and absurd: did you know people any better when you'd seen them eating? If that was the case, she didn't dare imagine the opinion they had of her at school, where the canteen, as far as she was concerned, was a place of torture and vomiting.

Plectrude said to herself that if *she* wanted to know someone, she would invite her to play. Wasn't it at play that people revealed themselves?

Nevertheless, Roselyne was invited to dinner, because that was the way adults did things. Everything went very well. Plectrude waited impatiently for the small talk to come to an end: she knew that she would be sleeping with her friend, in her bedroom, and that idea struck her as marvellous.

Darkness, finally.

'Are you afraid of the dark?' she said hopefully.

'Yes,' said Roselyne.

'I'm not!'

'I see monsters in the dark.'

'So do I. But I like that.'

'You like dragons?'

'Yes! And bats.'

'Doesn't it frighten you?'

'No. Because I'm their queen.'

'How do you know?'

'I decided.'

Roselyne thought this was an admirable explanation.

'I'm the queen of everything you see in the dark: jellyfish, crocodiles, snakes, spiders, sharks, dinosaurs, slugs, octopuses.'

'Don't they disgust you?'

'No. I think they're lovely.'

'So there isn't anything that disgusts you, then?'

'Yes, there is! Dried figs.'

'Dried figs aren't disgusting!'

'Do you eat them?'

'Yes.'

'Well don't, not if you love me.'

'Why not?'

'The salesgirls chew them and then put them back in the packet.'

'What are you on about?'

'Why do you think they're all crushed and horrible?'

'Is that true?'

'I swear. The salesgirls chew them up and then spit them back out again.'

'Ugh!'

'You see! There's nothing in the world more disgusting than dried figs.'

They swooned with a shared disgust that took them to seventh heaven. For a long time they detailed the repugnant aspects of this desiccated fruit, uttering cries of pleasure.

'I swear I'm never going to eat them ever again,' Roselyne said solemnly.

'Even under torture?'

'Even under torture!'

'And what if someone stuffs them into your mouth by force?'

'I swear I'll throw up!' the child declared, in the voice of a young bride.

That night elevated their friendship to the level of a mystery cult.

In class, Plectrude's status had changed. She had moved from the condition of pestiferous outcast to adulated best friend. At least if she had been adored by a clod of her own kind, she could have gone on being undesirable. But in the eyes of the pupils, Roselyne could do no wrong. Her sole defect, which consisted of being a new girl, was a very ephemeral stain on her character. From that time on they wondered if they hadn't been mistaken about Plectrude.

Obviously, these discussions never actually took place. The thoughts circulated in the collective unconscious of the class. Their impact was all the greater for it.

Certainly, Plectrude remained a dunce in sums and many other areas. But the children discovered that a weakness in certain subjects, particularly when it was taken to extremes, could sometimes have something admirable and heroic about it. Gradually they came to understand the charm of this form of subversion.

The teacher didn't seem to.

The parents were summoned again.

'With your permission, we are going to make your child undergo some tests.'

There was no way of refusing. Denis felt profoundly humiliated: they were saying his daughter was handicapped. Clémence was delighted: Plectrude was extraordinary. Even if they detected that the girl was mentally defective, she would take that as a sign that she was one of the elect.

So the child was subjected to all kinds of logical sequences, abstruse lists, geometrical figures containing irrelevant puzzles, formulae that were pompously called algorithms. She replied mechanically, as quickly as possible, in order to hide a violent desire to laugh.

Was it chance or the benefit of an absence of thought? She obtained a result so excellent that it astonished everyone. And thus it was that within the space of an hour, Plectrude rose from being a simpleton to being a genius.

'I'm not surprised,' her mother commented, vexed at her husband's amazement.

This change of terminology brought advantages, as the child soon became aware. Previously, when she couldn't work out an exercise, the teacher would give her a pained look, and the most hateful of the pupils laughed at her.

Now, when she couldn't get to the end of a simple task, the teacher contemplated her like the albatross in Baudelaire's poem: her massive intelligence prevented her from doing her calculations, and her fellow pupils were ashamed at stupidly reaching the solution.

Besides, since she really was intelligent, Plectrude wondered why she couldn't solve easy sums, while, during the tests, she had given correct answers to exercises that should have been beyond her.

She remembered that she had not been thinking at all during those tests, and concluded from this that the key to everything was absolute thoughtlessness.

From that point onwards, she took care not to think when a task was put in front of her, and to write down the first numbers that came into her head. Her results didn't get any better, but they didn't get any worse, either. Consequently, she decided to keep to this method, which, by virtue of being just as ineffective as the earlier one, was fantastically liberating. And that was how she became the most highly esteemed dunce in France.

It would all have been perfect had there not, at the end of each school year, been annoying formalities designed to select those who would have the good fortune to move to the next class up.

This time was a nightmare for Plectrude, who was only too well aware of the role of chance in these events. Fortunately, her reputation as a genius preceded her: when the teacher saw the incongruity of her results in mathematics, he concluded that the child might be right in another dimension, and wiped the slate. Or else he questioned the little girl about her reasoning, and what she said left him flabbergasted with incomprehension. She had learned to mimic what people thought was the language of a gifted girl. For example, at the end of a stream of utter gibberish, she would conclude with a limpid 'It's obvious.'

It wasn't obvious at all to the masters and mistresses. But they preferred not to boast about the fact, and awarded their pupil their *nihil obstat*.

Genius or not, the little girl had only one obsession: dancing.

The more she grew, the more amazed the dance teachers were by her gifts. She had virtuosity and grace, rigour and imagination, prettiness and a sense of the tragic, precision and spirit.

The best thing was that it was impossible not to see that she was happy dancing – prodigiously happy. Her delight at handing over her body to the great energy of dance was tangible. It was as though her soul had spent ten thousand years waiting just for that. The arabesque freed her from some mysterious internal tension.

What was more, she obviously had a feeling for theatre: the presence of an audience increased her talent, and the keener the eyes upon her, the more intensely she moved.

There was also the miracle of her slenderness, which would not leave her. Plectrude was, and remained, as thin as a figure in an Egyptian relief. Her weightlessness was an insult to the laws of gravity.

In the end, without consulting each other, her teachers all said the same thing about her: 'She has the eyes of a dancer.'

CLÉMENCE SOMETIMES HAD THE FEELING that too many fairies had leaned over the child's cradle: she was worried that she would end up with her attracting the thunderbolts of the gods.

Fortunately, her own children to the prodigy without any great difficulty. Plectrude had not encroached upon the territories of her two older sisters. Nicole was top of the class in science and physical education, Béatrice had a flair for maths and a knack for history. Perhaps out of instinctive diplomacy, the girl was useless in all these subjects – even in gymnastics, in which her dancing seemed to be of no help to her.

So Denis assigned access to a third of the universe to each of the girls. 'Nicole is going to be a scientist and an athlete: why not an astronaut? Béatrice will be an intellectual, her head peopled with numbers and facts: she'll assemble historical statistics. And Plectrude is an artist brimming over with charisma; she'll be a dancer or a political leader, or both at once.'

He concluded his prediction with an explosion of laughter, of pride rather than doubt. The children listened to him with pleasure, because his words were flattering; but the youngest could not help feeling slightly perplexed, both at these propositions which struck her as hostile to knowledge, and at her father's assurance.

Despite being only ten years old, and not advanced for her age, she had none the less understood one important thing: that people on this earth did not harvest what seemed their due.

Besides, being ten years old is the best thing that can happen to a human being. Especially a little dancer with all her art at her disposal.

Ten is the most sunlit point in childhood. There is no sign of adolescence visible on the horizon: nothing but mature childhood, already rich in long experience, without that feeling of loss that assaults you from the first hints of puberty onwards. At ten, you aren't necessarily happy, but you are certainly alive, more alive than anyone else.

Plectrude, at the age of ten, was a nucleus of intense vitality. She was at the summit of her reign. She ruled over her dancing school, of which she was the uncontested star, and was accepted as queen by girls of all ages. She ruled over her class of ten-year-olds, which threatened to become a dunceocracy since the pupil who was the most useless at maths, science, history, geography, gymnastics etc., was considered a genius.

She ruled over the heart of her mother, who nurtured an

infinite passion for her. And she ruled over Roselyne, whose love for her was matched only by her admiration.

Plectrude's triumph was not a crushing one. Her extraordinary status did not turn her into one of those stuck-up ten-year-old madams who think they are above the laws of friendship. She was devoted to Roselyne, and she worshipped her friend every bit as much as her Roselyne worshipped her.

An obscure prescience seemed to have warned her that she might lose her throne. This anxiety seemed all the more well founded since she remembered the time when she had been the laughing stock of the class.

Roselyne and Plectrude had already been married several times, most often to each other, but not necessarily. On some occasions they also married a boy from their class who, in the most fabulous ceremonies, was represented by his own ectoplasm, sometimes in the form of a scarecrow effigy, sometimes in the form of Roselyne or Plectrude disguised as a man – an opera hat was enough to effect the change of sex.

The identity of the husband, in fact, was of little importance. As long as the real or imaginary individual displayed no unacceptable vices (overeating, high-pitched voice or a propensity to begin his sentences with the words: 'D'you know what? . . .'), he was suitable. The purpose of the game was to create a nuptial dance, a kind of dance-play worthy of Lully, with songs improvised around lyrics that were as tragic as they could possibly be.

It was inevitable, in fact, that after all too brief a marriage, the husband turned into a bird or a toad, and the wife found herself locked up once more in a high tower with an impossible task to perform.

'Why is the ending always so sad?' Roselyne asked one day.

'Because it's much nicer that way,' Plectrude assured her.

That winter, the dancer invented a sublimely heroic game: it involved allowing yourself to be buried in snow, not moving and not putting up the slightest resistance.

'Making a snowman is too easy,' she had decreed. 'You have to *become* a snowman, standing under the snowflakes, or else a recumbent figure made of snow, lying down in a garden.'

Roselyne looked at her with sceptical admiration.

'You be the snowman and I'll be the recumbent figure,' Plectrude went on.

Her friend didn't dare voice her qualms. And the two girls found themselves beneath the snow, one lying on the ground and the other standing up. The standing one ceased to see the funny side very quickly. Her feet were cold, she wanted to move, she had no desire to become a living monument, and on top of that she was bored, because apart from being worthy statues, the two little girls had agreed to be silent.

The recumbent figure was exultant. It had kept its eyes open, as corpses do before third parties intervene. Lying on the ground, it had relinquished its body: it had parted company from the sensation of freezing cold, and from the physical fear of leaving its skin. All that remained was a face receptive to the forces of the sky.

Plectrude's ten-year-old femininity was not present, not that it would have been a burden: the recumbent figure had preserved only the very minimum of itself, in order to put up as little resistance as possible to the pale torrent of snowflakes.

Its wide-open eyes contemplated the most fascinating spectacle in the world: white, exploding death, sent down to it by the universe as a jigsaw puzzle, pieces detached from a single vast mystery.

Sometimes its eye studied its body, which was buried before its face was, because the clothes acted as a form of insulation. Then its eyes returned to the clouds again, and gradually the warmth faded from the figure's cheeks, and soon the shroud was able to deposit its first veil upon it, and the recumbent figure stopped smiling so as not to spoil its elegance.

A billion snowflakes later, the thin silhouette of the recumbent figure was almost indiscernible, barely a bump in the white amalgam of the garden.

The only cheating lay in blinking from time to time, and not always deliberately. This meant that the figure's eyes had preserved their access to the sky, and were still able to observe the slow, deadly cascade.

Air passed through the layer of ice, ensuring that the figure did not suffocate. The figure felt a tremendous, superhuman sense of something, a struggle with some unknown force, some unidentifiable angel – was the struggle with the snow, or with the recumbent figure? – but also of a remarkable serenity, of the most profound acceptance.

Where the snowman was concerned, on the other hand, things weren't quite working. Undisciplined, and unconvinced of the pertinence of the experiment, he couldn't stop moving. Besides, the upright posture was not so conducive to burial; and even less to submission.

Roselyne looked at the recumbent figure, wondering what she should do. She knew her friend was the kind to take things to their conclusion, and knew that she would forbid her to intervene on her behalf.

She had been instructed to remain silent, but she decided to be disobedient: 'Plectrude, can you hear me?'

There was no reply.

It could be that Plectrude, in her fury at the snowman's disobedience, had decided to punish him with silence. Such an attitude would have been entirely in line with her character.

It could also mean something very different.

A storm was raging in Roselyne's skull.

The snow lay thick on face of the recumbent figure. It couldn't shake it off, even by blinking. The openings which had, until then, been left free around the figure's eyes, closed over.

At first, the daylight still managed to pass through the veil, and the figure had the sublime vision of a dome of crystals a few millimetres away from its pupils: lovely as a trove of gemstones.

Soon the shroud grew opaque. Facing death, the figure found itself in darkness. The darkness held great fascinations: it was incredible to discover that such darkness reigned beneath such whiteness.

Gradually, the amalgam grew increasingly dense.

The recumbent figure noticed that the air was no longer filtering through. It wanted to get up, to free itself of its gag, but the layer of ice had frozen solid, forming an igloo in the exact proportions of its body, and it knew now that it was imprisoned: this would be its tomb.

Then the living person behaved like a living person: it screamed. Its cries were muffled by the centimetres of snow: all that emerged from the hillock was a barely audible moan. Finally, Roselyne heard the sound, and hurled herself on her friend, dragging her from her snowflake tomb, using her hands like a mechanical digger. The girl's blue face appeared, spectral in its beauty.

The survivor uttered a delirious cry: 'It was magnificent!'

'Why didn't you get up? You were dying!'

'Because I was trapped. The snow had frozen.'

'No it hadn't! I was able to pull it away with my hands!'

'Really? Then the cold must have made me too weak to move.'

She said that in such an offhand manner that Roselyne, perplexed, wondered whether she wasn't pretending. But no, she really was blue. On the other hand, you can't pretend to die.

Plectrude stood up and looked gratefully at the sky.

'What just happened to me was fantastic!'

'You're mad. I don't know if you realize that you wouldn't be alive without me.'

'Yes. Thanks, you've saved my life. That makes everything even more beautiful.'

'What on earth's beautiful about it?'

'Everything!'

The elated girl went home and suffered only a bad cold.

Her friend thought she had got off lightly. Her admiration for the dancer didn't stop her from thinking she was losing her marbles: she always had to put her own life centre-stage, she had to surround herself with grandeur, to arrange the most sublime dangers where all was calm, and then to emerge from them like a miracle survivor.

Roselyne could never shake off the suspicion that Plectrude had remained trapped beneath her snowy shroud on purpose: she knew her friend's predilections, and knew that she would have thought the story much less admirable if she had got out of it all by herself. In order to comply with her own aesthetic notions, she had chosen to wait to be saved. And she wondered whether Plectrude would not have been capable of allowing herself to die rather than compromise the heroic rules her character imposed upon her.

Certainly, she had never had any confirmation of her prognostications. Sometimes she tried to prove the opposite to herself: 'After all, she was the one who called me for help. If she really had been insane, she wouldn't have done that.'

But other troubling events happened, and intrigued her. When they were waiting together for the bus, Plectrude would often stand in the road and stay there even when cars came towards her. When that happened, Roselyne would tug her back bossily on to the pavement. At that very moment, the dancer wore an utterly rapturous expression.

Her friend didn't know what to think. That annoyed her a little.

One day, she resolved not to intervene, just to see. She saw.

A lorry was heading straight for Plectrude, who stayed in the road anyway. She must have known it was coming. And yet she didn't move. Roselyne realized that her friend was gazing straight into her eyes. None the less, she repeated this inner leitmotif to herself: 'Let her sort it out, let her sort it out.'

The lorry was getting dangerously close.

'Look out!' yelled Roselyne.

The dancer stood motionless, staring into her friend's eyes.

At the very last second, Roselyne grabbed her furiously by the arm and dragged her out of the road.

Plectrude's mouth was contorted with delight.

'You saved me,' she said with a sigh of ecstasy.

'You're completely mad,' her friend raged. 'That lorry could very easily have crushed us both. Would you have wanted me to die for your sake?'

'No,' said the child, astonished, apparently never having considered that possibility.

'So never do it again!'

She took the warning.

❤

In her own mind, Plectrude ran through the scene in the snow a thousand times.

Her version was very different from Roselyne's.

In point of fact, she was so much the dancer that she lived out every last scene of her life as though it were a ballet. Her choreographies ensured that a sense of tragedy appeared at every turning: what would have been grotesque in everyday life was not so in opera, even less so in dance.

'I gave myself to the snow in the garden, I lay down beneath it and it built a cathedral around me, I saw it slowly raising the walls, then the vaults, I was the recumbent figure with the cathedral all to myself, then the doors closed again and death came in search of me, white and gentle at first, then black and violent, it was going to take me away when my guardian angel came to save me at the very last minute.'

As to being saved, it was better if it happened at the very last minute: it was much nicer that way. Anything less would have been a failure of taste.

Roselyne didn't know she was playing the part of guardian angel.

PLECTRUDE TURNED TWELVE. It was the first time that a birthday had given her a vague twinge in the heart. Until that point, another year had always seemed like a good thing: it was a motif of pride, a heroic step towards a future that was bound to be beautiful. Twelve was like a boundary: the last innocent birthday.

She refused to think about thirteen. It sounded horrible. The world of teenagers left her as cold as anything could. Thirteen was sure to be full of break-ups, illness, gloom, acne, first periods, bras and other horrors.

Twelve was the last birthday when she could feel sheltered from the calamities of adolescence. With delight she stroked her torso, flat as a parquet floor.

The dancer went and snuggled in her mother's arms. Her mother fussed over her, cosseted her, said loving little words to her, rubbed her back and her arms – she lavished on her the thousand exquisite signs of affection that the very best mothers give to their daughters.

Plectrude loved that. She closed her eyes with pleasure;

no love, she thought, could give her such pleasure as her mother's did. The idea of being in a boy's arms didn't fire her imagination. Being in the arms of Clémence was the absolute. Yes, but would her mother still love her as much when she was a spotty adolescent? The idea terrified her. She didn't dare ask the question.

From that point onwards, Plectrude cultivated her childhood. She was like a landowner who has had an enormous estate at his disposal for many years and, following some disaster, has been left with only a little plot. Making a virtue of a necessity, she lavished care and love upon her patch of land, pampering the rare flowers of childhood that she was still able to water.

She wore her hair in plaits or pigtails, she dressed only in dungarees, she walked around clutching a teddy bear to her heart and sat on the ground to do up her Kickers.

She didn't have to force herself to behave like a child: she just let herself drift to the side of herself that she liked best, aware that she wouldn't be able to do so the following year.

Such rules might seem strange. They aren't strange to children and little adolescents, who minutely observe which of their playmates are advanced and which of them are lagging behind. Their admiration is as paradoxical as their contempt. Those who play up either their precocity or their late development attract opprobrium, punishment and ridicule or, more rarely, a heroic reputation.

Take a second-year or third-year class, and ask any girl in that class which of her classmates are already wearing bras: you will be astonished by the exactitude of the reply.

In Plectrude's class – she was already in the second year – there were some who mocked her pigtails, but they were the girls who were advanced in terms of bra-wearing, and that in turn brought them more derision than it did praise: one might well have imagined that their mockery was a form of compensation for their jealousy over the dancer's flat torso.

As to the boys, their attitude towards the bra pioneers was ambiguous: they ogled them, while at the same time saying the most contemptuous things about them. That, incidentally, is a habit that the members of the male sex preserve throughout the whole of their lives: they make a point of slandering the very things that haunt their masturbatory obsessions.

The first manifestations of sexuality were appearing on the second-year horizon; Plectrude saw that she must arm herself with an emphatic form of innocence. She could not put her fear into words: she knew only that if some of her fellow pupils were already prepared for 'strange things', she was not. Unconsciously she set about warning the others of this, by giving powerful reinforcement to her childhood state.

In November, a new arrival was announced.

Plectrude liked new pupils. Would Roselyne have become her best friend if she hadn't been a new girl, five years before? The little dancer was forever linking up with more or less alarmed strangers.

The attitude among most of the children, whether conscious or not, was to show no mercy towards the new boy or new girl: the slightest of their 'differences' (such as peeling an orange with a knife, or saying 'poo!' rather than the classic 'shit!'), provoked whoops of outrage.

As to Plectrude, she was delighted by odd behaviour: she felt the enthusiasm of an ethnologist faced with the customs of an exotic tribe. 'That way of peeling his orange with a knife is rather elegant, rather astonishing!' or, '"Poo"; how very unexpected!' She went up to the new pupils with the welcoming generosity of a Tahitian receiving European sailors, brandishing her smile rather than a garland of hibiscus flowers.

The arrival of a new pupil was particularly heart-wrenching when he was so incongruous as to turn up in the middle of the school year rather than joining the rest of the flock in September.

This was the case with the new boy. The little dancer was already extremely well disposed towards him by the time he came into the classroom. Plectrude's face froze in a mixture of horror and admiration.

His name was Mathieu Saladin. He was found a seat at the back, near the radiator.

Plectrude didn't listen to a word that the teacher said. She was feeling something extraordinary. She had a pain in her thorax, and she loved it. A thousand times she wanted to turn round to look at the boy. As a general rule, she was happy to gawp at people to the point of rudeness. This time she couldn't.

At last it was break time. Ordinarily, the little dancer

would have walked up to the new boy with a luminous smile to put him at his ease. This time, she remained desperately motionless.

The other pupils, however, remained loyal to their habits of hostility.

'So this new boy, did he fight in the Vietnam war, or what?'

'Let's call him Scarface.'

Plectrude felt anger welling up in her. It was all she could do not to yell, 'Shut up! It's a wonderful scar! I've never seen such a sublime boy!'

Mathieu Saladin's mouth was split in two by a long perpendicular scar, well stitched but visible. It was much too large to suggest the post-operative mark of a harelip.

The dancer knew without hesitation: it was a fencing wound. The boy's surname, she thought, evoked the stories of the *Thousand and One Nights*, and in fact she was not mistaken in this, for the name was of distantly Persian origin. Henceforth it went without saying that the boy possessed a curved sabre. He must have used it to carve up some evil crusader who had come to claim the tomb of Christ. Before biting the dust, the Christian knight, in a vengeful gesture of dreadful petty-mindedness (because, after all, Mathieu Saladin had been content to cut him into pieces, which was considered perfectly normal at the time), had thrown his sword right into his mouth, forever inscribing their battle upon his face.

The new boy had regular, classic features, both amiable and impassive. It made his scar stand out all the more. Plectrude, completely silent, marvelled at what she was feeling.

'So how are you going to welcome the new boy: the way you usually do?' said Roselyne.

The dancer thought her silence risked attracting attention. She summoned her courage, took a deep breath and walked towards the boy, smiling tensely.

At that very moment he was with an awful lout called Didier, a boy who was repeating a year, and who was trying to monopolize Mathieu Saladin by boasting about having a man with a scarred face among his relations.

'Hello, Mathieu,' she mumbled. 'My name is Plectrude.'

'Hello,' he replied, soberly and politely.

Normally, she would have added a tart and pleasant formula along the lines of: 'Welcome among us,' or: 'I hope you'll enjoy yourself here.' Now she couldn't say a word. She turned on her heels and went back to her seat.

'A funny name, but a very pretty girl,' commented Mathieu Saladin.

'Yeah, whatever,' murmured Didier, acting blasé. 'If it's totty you're after, don't go for the little kids. Come over here and look at Muriel. I call her "Melons".'

'I can see that,' agreed the new boy.

'Do you want me to introduce you?'

Before he even had a reply, Didier took the boy by the shoulder and led him up to the creature with the impressive torso. The dancer didn't hear what they were saying. She had a bitter taste in her mouth.

The night after that first encounter, Plectrude addressed herself as follows:

'He's for me. He's mine. He doesn't know it, but he belongs to me. I promise myself: Mathieu Saladin is for me. I don't care if it's in a month or twenty years. I swear it.'

She repeated this to herself for hours, like an incantatory formula, with an assurance that she would not regain for a very long time.

The next day she had to face the facts: the new boy didn't have so much as a glance for her. She darted her marvellous eyes at him, and he noticed nothing at all.

'If he hadn't been injured, he would be simply handsome. With that scar, he's magnificent,' she said to herself, again and again.

Although she wasn't aware of the fact, this obsession with Mathieu's battle-scar was rich in meaning. Plectrude believed herself to be the real daughter of Clémence and Denis, and knew nothing of the circumstances of her real birth. She was unaware of the extraordinary violence that had greeted her arrival among the living.

However, there must have been a region somewhere in her inner darkness that was drenched in that climate of murder and blood, because what she felt as she contemplated the boy's scar was as profound as an ancestral wound.

One consolation: if he was not interested in her, she had to acknowledge that he wasn't interested in anyone else either. Mathieu Saladin was even-tempered, his features were not mobile, his face expressed nothing but a neutral politeness which applied equally to everyone. He was tall, very thin and very frail. His eyes had the wisdom of those who have suffered.

Whenever he was asked a question, he took time to reflect, and his answers were always intelligent. Plectrude had never met a boy so far from being stupid.

He was neither especially good nor especially bad in any subject. In every area he reached the level required, which meant that he didn't attract attention.

The little dancer, whose marks had stayed dreadful over the years, admired him for that. She was still happy to have gained sympathy and a certain esteem among her peers: had she not done so, she would have had even more trouble enduring the reactions that her answers provoked.

'What makes you come out with such nonsense?' some of her teachers asked, dismayed by the things she said.

She wanted to tell them she wasn't doing it on purpose. But she had a feeling that that would make her case even worse. If you made the whole class giggle, you might as well claim it was premeditated.

The teachers thought she was proud of the reactions of the class, and that she solicited them intentionally. The opposite was the case. When her gaffes provoked general hilarity, she wanted to sink into the floor.

One example among several: when the class was discussing the city of Paris and its historical monuments, Plectrude was asked about the Louvre. The answer required was the Arc de Triomphe. The girl replied: 'The Ark of the Covenant.'

The class applauded this new piece of inanity with the enthusiasm of an audience greeting its comic.

Plectrude was at a loss. Her eyes sought the face of Mathieu Saladin: she saw that he was laughing fit to bust, although he was doing so affectionately. She sighed with a mixture of relief and contempt: relief, because things might have been worse; contempt, because his expression was very different from the one she had hoped to provoke in him.

'If only he could see me dance!' she thought.

Alas, how could she reveal her talent? Anyway, there was no question of her going up to him and telling him point blank that she was the star of her generation.

The worst of it was that the new boy spent almost all his time with Didier. There was no point in banking on that fool to tell him: Didier cared as much about Plectrude as he did about the year 1940. He only ever talked about stupid magazines, football, cigarettes and beer. Being a year older than everyone else, he acted the grown-up, claiming that he shaved, which was hard to believe, and bragging of his success with third- and fourth-year girls.

You might have wondered what Mathieu Saladin saw in the company of such a pathetic character. Basically, he saw nothing at all: he spent his time with Didier because Didier was willing to spend time with him. He didn't care a jot about Didier. He wasn't bothered by him either way.

One day she summoned a fantastic amount of courage, and went to speak to her hero during break time. Her plan was to ask him who his favourite singer was.

He replied that he wasn't especially convinced by any particular singer, and that for that reason he had set up a rock group with a few friends.

'We meet in my parents' garage to make the sort of music that people would like to hear.'

Plectrude almost fainted with admiration. She was too much in love to have any presence of mind, so she didn't say what she would like to have said: 'I'd like to hear you and your group play.'

She didn't say a word. From this Mathieu Saladin concluded that she wasn't interested, so he didn't invite her to his garage. If he had done, she wouldn't have wasted seven years of her life. For the want of a nail the horse was lost . . .

'And what sort of music do you like?' the boy asked.

It was a disaster. She was still at the age when you listen to the same music as your parents. Denis and Clémence loved the good old French chansons, people like Barbara, Léo Ferré, Jacques Brel, Serge Reggiani, Charles Trenet: if she had mentioned one of those names, it would have been an excellent reply and highly respectable.

But Plectrude was ashamed of herself: 'You're twelve years old and you haven't even got tastes of your own. You aren't going to tell him that: he'd work out that it's your parents' music.'

Alas, she had no idea who the good late-seventies singers were. She knew only a single name, and that was the one that she uttered:

'Dave.'

Mathieu Saladin's reaction wasn't really ill-meant: he burst out laughing. 'Goodness but she's a funny one!' he thought.

She could have extricated herself from this hilarity, but she experienced it as a humiliation. She turned on her heels and left. 'I'm never going to speak to him again,' she said to herself.

This was the start of a period of decline for her. Her school marks, which had always been bad, started becoming execrable. Her reputation as a genius, which had so troubled her teachers up until then, was no longer enough.

Plectrude put heart and soul into it: she appeared to have chosen educational suicide. As though intoxicated, she went crashing into the boundaries of incompetence and sent them flying.

If she gave horrendous answers to her teachers' questions, she wasn't doing it on purpose: her only choice was to stop imposing checks on herself. From now on she would let herself go, she would say whatever her inner dunce dictated: no more, no less. Her intention was not to attract attention (although, to be honest, she didn't mind that), but to be rejected, driven out, expelled like the foreign body that she was. The rest of the class heard her coming out with monstrosities by turn geographical ('the source of the Nile is in the Mediterranean and it doesn't flow into anything'), geometrical ('a right angle is ninety degrees Celsius'), orthographical ('the past participle agrees with women unless there's a man in the group'), historical ('Louis XIV became a Protestant when he married Edith of Nantes') and biological ('cats have nubile eyes and nyctalopic claws') with admiration.

Admiration which was, indeed, shared by the girl herself. In fact, it was with a degree of ecstatic astonishment that she heard herself coming out with such blunders: she couldn't hold back so many surrealistic pearls, and became aware of the infinity within her.

As to the other pupils, they had come to the conclusion that Plectrude's attitude was one of pure provocation. Every time the teacher asked her a question, they held their breath, then marvelled at the natural aplomb with which she uttered her gems. They thought her aim was to ridicule the educational institution, and they applauded her courage.

Her reputation passed beyond the classroom walls. At break time, everyone in the school came to ask the second-year pupils about 'Plectrude's latest'. Her heroic deeds were related like an epic tale.

The conclusion was always the same:

'She's going too far!'

'YOU'RE GOING A BIT FAR, AREN'T YOU?' her father said angrily when he saw her report.

'I don't want to go to school any more, Papa. It's not for me.'

'We're not having this!'

'I want to be a "petit rat" at the Paris Opéra.'

Her words didn't fall on deaf ears.

'She's quite right!' said Clémence.

'So you're defending her as well?'

'Of course! Our Plectrude's a genius at dancing! At her age she's got to devote herself to it body and soul! Why should she go on wasting her time with past participles?'

That same day, Clémence phoned the school of the 'petits rats'.

The girl's usual dancing school was very keen on the idea:

'We were hoping you'd decide on something like that! She's made for it!'

They wrote letters of recommendation for her, speaking of her as the future Pavlova.

She was summoned by the Opéra to sit an exam. Clémence shrieked when she got the letter calling her in, even though it meant nothing at all.

On the agreed day, Plectrude and her mother took the RER train into the city. Clémence's heart was pounding even more than the child's when they reached the école des rats.

Two weeks later, Plectrude received the letter admitting her to the school. It was the loveliest day of her mother's life.

In September, she would start at the Opéra school, where she would be a boarder. The little girl was living a dream. A great destiny was opening up before her.

This was April. Denis insisted that she should finish her school year and collect her marks: 'That way you'll be able to say you completed the third year.'

The child thought that was a mean and ridiculous trick on his part. None the less, out of affection for her father, she put her back into it and rightly obtained the results she needed. Now she was in favour with everyone.

The whole college knew why she was going, and was very proud of her. Even the teachers who had thought her a nightmare declared that they had always sensed the child's 'genius'.

The students praised her grace, the dinner ladies lauded her lack of appetite, the teacher of physical education (a field in which the dancer was outstandingly dreadful) spoke of her suppleness and the delicacy of her muscles; and to cap it all, those pupils who had never stopped hating her since reception year prided themselves on being her friends.

Alas, the only member of the class whom the girl would have liked to impress showed nothing but polite admiration. If she had known Mathieu Saladin better, she would have known why his face was so impassive.

In fact he was thinking, 'Well, fuck. And there I was thinking I had another five years to achieve my goal! And she's going to be a star! I'm never going to see her again, that's for sure. If she were even a friend, I'd have an excuse to meet up with her in the future. But I've never really formed a friendship with her, and I'm not going to behave like one of those oafs who pretend they adore a girl because they know what they're going to get in the end.'

On the final day of class, Mathieu Saladin bade her a chilly goodbye.

'He's still glad I'm leaving the school,' the dancer sighed. 'I'm never going to see him again, and who knows, maybe I won't think about him so much. He couldn't care less that I'm going!'

That summer, they didn't go away on holiday: the école des rats was expensive. The phone in the flat never stopped ringing: it was a neighbour, an uncle, a friend, a colleague, wanting to come and gaze upon this phenomenon.

'And she's beautiful as well!' they exclaimed when they saw her.

Plectrude couldn't wait to go to boarding school so that she could get away from the constant queue of gaping onlookers.

To escape the boredom, she ruminated on her amorous woes. She climbed to the top of her special tree, throwing her arms around its trunk and closing her eyes. She told herself stories and the cherry tree became Mathieu Saladin.

She opened them again and became aware of how stupid she was being. She fumed: 'It's so stupid to be twelve and a half, and for everyone to like you except Mathieu Saladin!'

In her bed at night, the stories she told herself grew much more intense: she and Mathieu Saladin were trapped in a barrel that was being thrown over the Niagara Falls. The barrel crashed open on some rocks, and by turns it was either Plectrude or Mathieu who was wounded or lifeless, and who had to be saved.

There was something to be said for both versions. When she was the one being rescued, she loved him diving to look for her at the bottom of the maelstrom, wrapping her in his arms to bring her back to life and then, on the shore, giving her artificial respiration; when it was he who was injured, she pulled him from the water and talked to herself about his wounds, licking the blood from them, rejoicing over new scars that were going to make him even more handsome.

By the end she felt shivers of desire that drove her out of her mind.

❤

She waited for the new term as though for a liberation. It was an incarceration.

She knew that the école des rats was run with a rod of iron. But what she discovered there went far beyond her wildest predictions.

Plectrude had always been the thinnest person in every group of human beings of which she had been a member. Here, she was one of the 'normal' ones. The ones who were called 'thin' would have been called skeletal anywhere outside of the boarding school. As to those who, in the outside world, would have been considered to have commonplace proportions, within these walls they were mocked as the 'fat cows'.

The first day was worthy of a butcher's shop. A kind of thin, old sausage-maker came to view the pupils as though they were cuts of meat. She separated them into three categories, to whom she addressed these words:

'Thin ones, that's fine, you keep on like that. Normal ones, OK, but I've got my eye on you. Fat cows, either you lose weight or you go: there's no room for sows in here.'

These sweet words were greeted with mirth by the thin ones: they looked like laughing corpses. 'They're monstrous,' thought Plectrude.

One 'fat cow', a pretty little girl with a perfectly normal figure, burst into tears. The old woman came and yelled at her:

'There's no point snivelling in here. If you want to go on stuffing your fat face with barley sugars while you hide in your mother's skirts, no one here's holding you back.'

Then the young pieces of meat were weighed and measured. Plectrude, who was going to be thirteen in a month's time, was five feet two and weighed six and a half stone, which wasn't much, especially bearing in mind that it was all muscle; after all, she was a dancer who took good care of herself. None the less, she was informed that this was a 'maximum that should not be exceeded'.

That first day at the école des rats gave all the little girls a sense that they had been brutally evicted from childhood: the previous day, their bodies had still been much-loved plants, watered and cherished. Their growth was wished for like marvellous natural phenomena, with many fine days to come; their families were gardens where the soil was rich, and where life was slow and cosy. And then, from one day to the next, they were uprooted from the damp earth, and found themselves in a desiccated world, where the fierce eye of an oriental plant-specialist decreed that a particular stem would have to be lengthened, a particular root would have to be lopped, and that this would happen whether they wanted it to or not because they had developed the special techniques required over the course of time.

Here, there was no tenderness in the eyes of the adults: merely a scalpel to slice away the last flesh of childhood. The little girls had just travelled instantly through the centuries and through space: in only a few seconds they had passed from the end of the second millennium in France to medieval China.

It would be understating the case to say that the school was ruled with a rod of iron. Training began early in the morning and ended late at night, with barely noticeable interruptions for a meal that didn't deserve the name, and for a slot of study during which the pupils savoured the relaxation of their bodies so deeply that they forgot the intellectual effort required of them.

On this diet, all the girls grew thinner, including the ones who were too thin already. The latter, far from worrying about it as right-minded people might have done, rejoiced. You can never be too skeletal.

But contrary to what the first day had suggested, weight was not the chief concern. Their bodies were so exhausted by the endless hours of exercise that their sole obsession was to sit down. The moments when you didn't use your muscles seemed like a miracle.

From the moment she got up, Plectrude waited to go to bed. The moment when she consigned her aching and exhausted carcase to bed, to leave it there for the night, was so voluptuous that she could think of nothing else. This was the only relaxation that the little girls had. Meals, on the other hand, were times of anguish. The teachers had so demonized food that it appeared highly tempting, mediocre though it might have been. The children anticipated it with dread, disgusted by the desire it aroused in them. A single swallowed mouthful was a mouthful too many.

Very quickly, Plectrude started wondering about things. She had come to this establishment to become a dancer, not to lose her taste in life to the extent of having no higher ideal than sleep. Here, she worked on her dancing from morning till evening, without having a sense that dancing was what she was doing: she was like a writer forced not to write, and instead to study grammar incessantly. Certainly, grammar is essential, but only if writing is the end in view: deprived of its purpose, it is a sterile code. Plectrude had never felt less like a dancer than she had since coming to the école des rats. In the ballet classes that she had attended in previous years, there was room for little choreographies. Here all they did was exercises, full stop. The barre started looking like the bars of a jail.

Her perplexity seemed to be shared by many of the pupils. None of them spoke of it, but discouragement was felt spreading among the children none the less.

Some girls left, and the authorities seemed to have been hoping that they would. These defections led to others. This spontaneous shedding of surplus weight enchanted the teachers and wounded Plectrude, for whom each departure was like a bereavement.

Inevitably, she herself was tempted to leave. What stopped her was the faint sense that her mother would be angry with her, and that even her excellent explanations would be of no use.

It was clear that the people in charge of the school were waiting for a predetermined list of people to leave, for, from one day to the next, their attitude changed. The pupils were called to a larger room than usual, where they heard this speech:

'You must have noticed that many pupils have left the school over the last little while. We would not go as far as to say that we deliberately provoked them to go, but we will not be so hypocritical as to regret that they did.'

There was a silence, the sole purpose of which was doubtless to make the children uneasy.

'By leaving, those girls proved that they did not really want to dance; more precisely, they have shown that they lacked the patience that a true dancer needs to have. Are you aware what some of these silly geese said when they told us they were going? That they had come to dance, and that we did no dancing here. What on earth did they imagine? That they would be interpreting *Swan Lake* for us the day after tomorrow?'

Plectrude remembered an expression of her mother's: 'get your retaliation in first'. Yes, that's what it was: the teachers were busy getting their retaliation in first.

'Dancing is something you must deserve. Dancing – dancing on a stage in front of an audience – is the greatest joy in the world. To tell the truth, even without the audience, even without the stage, dancing is absolute intoxication. Such profound bliss is justification for the cruellest sacrifices. The education that we give you here presents dance for what it is: not the means, but the reward. It would be immoral to allow pupils to dance when they didn't deserve to. Eight hours a day at the barre and a famine diet will seem harsh only to those without sufficient desire to dance. So, those who still wish to leave, let them go!'

No one else went. The message had been received loud and clear. You can accept the severest forms of discipline as long as they have been explained to you properly.

The reward came: they danced.

To be sure, it wasn't much. But for the girls the mere fact of leaving the barre to launch themselves into the centre of the room with everyone watching, twirling around for a few moments and feeling the extent to which their bodies had mastered their steps was, utterly intoxicating. If ten seconds could give so much pleasure, the girls could hardly imagine what they would feel if they danced for two hours.

For the first time, Plectrude felt sorry for Roselyne, who hadn't been admitted to the école des rats. She would only ever be an ordinary young girl for whom dancing would be a diversion. Now, Plectrude blessed her teachers' harshness, for having taught her that this art was a religion.

What had shocked her before seemed normal now. It seemed normal that they should be starved, that they should exhaust themselves at the barre by going over their technical exercises for hours at a stretch, that they were insulted, that children without a hint of plumpness were mocked as fat cows. It all seemed quite acceptable.

There was much else which was even worse, and which had initially made her feel as though she were witnessing crimes against human rights, but which now no longer revolted her. Those girls who displayed the signs of puberty earlier than the others were forced to swallow forbidden pills that blocked certain adolescent changes. Having carried out a secret little survey, Plectrude noticed that no one had periods at the école des rats, not even in the classes higher up the school.

She had had a secret talk about it with an older girl, who had told her, 'For most pupils those pills aren't even necessary. Under-nourishment is enough to obstruct the menstrual cycle and the physical modifications that come with the arrival of the first period. But there are some hard cases who still manage to enter puberty in spite of these privations. They have to take the famous pill that stops menstruation. The tampon is an object that you won't find in the school.'

'Are there no girls who have their periods in secret?'

'You're crazy! They know it's not in their interest. They're the ones who ask for the pill.'

At the time, Plectrude had been scandalized by that conversation. Now she accepted the worst manipulations, she found the establishment's Spartan laws quite magnificent.

Her spirit had been subjugated, literally: she was now beneath the teachers' yoke, she agreed with them on everything.

Fortunately the voice of her childhood, still nearby and more knowledgeably rebellious than that of adolescence, saved her by whispering healthily outrageous remarks to her: 'Do you know why this place is called the "école des rats"? They say it's after the pupils, but it's really after the teachers. Yes, they are rats, nasty gnarly rats with big teeth to gnaw the flesh from the bodies of the ballerinas. We at least deserve some credit for being passionate about dance, when that passion is what they lack: what interests them, good rats that they are, is just to rat on us, they want to eat us up. Rats are misers, and not only where money's concerned, oh no! Miserly with beauty, miserly with pleasure, with life and even with dance! You think they love dance! They are its worst enemies! They are chosen for their hatred of dance, deliberately, because if they loved it, that would make life far too easy for us. Loving what your teacher loves would be too natural. Here, they demand something superhuman of us: they demand that we sacrifice ourselves for an art that our masters hate that is, betrayed a hundred times a day by their small-mindedness. Dance is spirit, grace, generosity, absolute talent – the very opposite of the rat mentality.'

The dictionary supplied her with the nourishment that she lacked. Plectrude read with appetite and delectation: 'gutter rat, dirty rat, rat-faced, rat fink'. Yes, really, the school lived up to its name.

But there was a real plan involved in choosing wretched teachers. The institution thought, not without reason, that it would have been immoral to encourage the ballerinas. Dance, if it was to be total art, required the investment of the whole being. So the children's motivation had to be tested by undermining their ideal to its very foundations. Those who gave in could never have the mental stature of a star. Such procedures, monstrous though they were, were based on sound ethical principles.

But the teachers didn't know this. They were not aware of the supreme mission of their sadism, and exercised it simply out of a desire to hurt.

And thus it was that in secret, Plectrude also learned to dance against them.

WITHIN THREE MONTHS she lost eleven pounds. She was delighted. Particularly in that she had noticed an extraordinary phenomenon: in passing below the symbolic bar of six and a half stone, she had not merely lost weight, she had also lost her feelings.

Mathieu Saladin: that name which had once sent her into a trance now left her completely cold. But she hadn't seen the boy again, or had any news of him: so he hadn't been able to disappoint her. Neither had she met any other boys to take her mind off the boy she loved.

And it was not the passing of time that had made her cold. Three months wasn't long. And on top of that, she had been studying herself too closely not to notice the connection between cause and effect: every ounce she lost took with it a part of her love. She didn't regret it, on the contrary: to be able to regret it, she would have had to have some feelings left. She rejoiced at having rid herself of this double burden: the eleven pounds and a cumbersome passion.

Plectrude promised herself that she would remember this great law: love, regret, desire, infatuation – such idiocies were illnesses secreted by bodies that weighed more than six and a half stone.

If by some mischance she acquired such obesity again and if, in consequence, feelings started tormenting her heart once more, she would know the remedy for this ludicrous pathology: to stop eating, to allow herself to get below the six-and-a-half-stone bar.

When you weighed five and a half stone, life was different: the obsession lay in conquering the physical ordeals of the day, distributing your energy in such a way as to have enough left over for eight hours of exercise, courageously confronting the temptations of mealtimes, proud of your exhaustion – to dance, all in all, when you deserved to.

Dancing was Plectrude's sole transcendence. It fully justified this arid existence. Putting one's health on the line meant nothing at all as long as one could know the incredible sensation of taking flight.

There is a widespread misunderstanding about classical dance. For many, it is only a ludicrous universe of tutus and pink slippers, *à pointe* mannerisms and aerial soppiness. The worst thing is that it's true. It is all those things.

But it isn't just those things. Strip ballet of its sentimental affectations, its tulle, its academicism and its romantic chignons: you will discover that something remains, and that that something is hugely important. The proof of this is that the best modern dancers are recruited at the classical school.

For the Holy Grail of ballet is flight. No teacher would dream of putting it like that, for fear of sounding like a complete lunatic. But no one who has learned the technique of the *sissone*, the *entrechat*, the *grand jeté en avant*, could have any doubts on the matter: what they are trying to teach is the art of flying.

If the barre exercises are so tiresome, it's because the barre is a perch. When you dream of flying off, you are furious at being moored for hours on end to a piece of wood, when you can feel in your limbs the appeal of flying freely in the air.

In point of fact the barre corresponds to the training that fledglings receive in the nest: they are taught to spread their wings before they come to use them. For fledglings, a few hours is all it takes. But if a human being comes up with the unlikely project of changing species and learning to fly, it seems quite normal and necessary to devote several years of exhausting exercises to achieving that goal.

The reward will be far beyond all expectations the moment the dancer is allowed to leave the perch – the barre – and rocket into space. The sceptical spectator may not be able to see what happens in the body of the classical dancer at that precise moment: it is true madness. And the fact that this insanity respects a code and an iron discipline does nothing to detract from the deranged aspect of the whole business: classical ballet is the set of techniques designed to present as possible and reasonable the idea of human flight. Consequently, why would one be surprised by the grotesque and gothic attire in which the dance is practised? Could one expect such a demented project to be adopted by people of sound mind?

This lengthy interpolation is directed at all those who see the ballet as nothing but a source of amusement. They are right to be amused, but let them go beyond their laughter: within classical dance there also lurks a fearsome ideal.

And the ravages that this ideal can wreak upon a young mind are equivalent to those of a hard drug.

At Christmas, they had short holidays at home.

No pupil at the école des rats looked forward to these with any great excitement. On the contrary, the prospect filled them all with apprehension. Holidays: what possible point could there be in those? They had been justified from the time when life's purpose was pleasure, but that period, childhood, had come and gone: now, the sole meaning of existence was dance.

And family life, composed essentially of meals and flabbiness, was in direct contradiction of their new obsession.

Plectrude told herself that this too was a sign of leaving childhood: not looking forward to the coming of Christmas. It was the first time that had happened to her. She had been right, the previous year, to fear turning thirteen. She had really changed.

Everyone noticed it. They were struck by her thinness: her mother was the only one to be pleased. Denis, Nicole, Béatrice and Roselyne, who had been invited over, all disapproved.

'You've got a face like a razor blade.'

'She's a dancer,' protested Clémence. 'You couldn't have expected her to come back to us with big round cheeks.

You're very beautiful, my darling.'

Apart from her thinness, a more profound change left them even more perplexed because they couldn't put a name to it. Perhaps it was so sinister that they simply didn't dare to express it in words: Plectrude had lost a lot of her freshness. She had always been a laughing little girl, but now she lacked the spirit they all remembered in her.

'It must be the shock of coming home,' Denis thought.

But the impression grew stronger with the passing of the days. It was as though the dancer was absent: her apparent kindness did little to conceal her indifference.

As to mealtimes, they seemed to be a torment to her. Her family was used to her eating very little; now she really ate nothing at all, and the rest of the family felt tense until they had left the table.

If her relatives had been able to see what was happening in Plectrude's head, they would have been even more worried than they already were.

At first, on the day of her arrival, they had all struck her as obese. Even Roselyne, a slim adolescent, seemed enormous to her. She wondered how they could bear to have such huge bellies. She particularly wondered how they could bear to lead such vain lives, that great softness, spreading everywhere, leading nowhere. She blessed her harsh existence and all its privations: she at least was heading somewhere. It wasn't as though she was devoted to the cult of suffering, but she did need a meaning in her life: in that respect, she was already an adolescent.

❤

When they were alone, Roselyne told her all about what had happened to her classmates. She was breathless and excited: 'And guess what! Well, Vanessa's going out with Fred; yes, really, that fourth-year guy!'

She was very quickly disappointed with her lack of success.

'You were in their class for longer than I was – don't you care what's happening to them?'

'Don't take it the wrong way. If you knew how remote all that is from me at the moment.'

'Even Mathieu Saladin?' asked Roselyne, who had keen antennae for the past but not for the present.

'Of course,' Plectrude said wearily.

'You weren't always like this.'

'That's the truth.'

'Are there any boys at your school?'

'No. They take their classes separately. You never see them.'

'Just girls, then? What absolute hell!'

'You know, we haven't got time to think about such things.'

Plectrude didn't have the courage to launch into her explanations about the barrier separating those who weighed more than six and a half from those who weighed less, but she was more conscious of the truth of it than ever before. What the hell did she care about those ridiculous high-school flirtations? She felt even sorrier for Roselyne now that she was wearing a bra.

'Do you want me to show you?'

'What?'

'My bra. You haven't stopped staring at it all the time I've been talking to you.'

Roselyne lifted up her T-shirt. Plectrude shrieked with horror.

Deep down, the girl who had learned to dance against her teachers also learned to live against her family. She said nothing, but she studied her relations with consternation: 'How they all slump! As though they'd been defeated by the laws of gravity! Life has got to be better than that.'

She found that their lives, unlike her own, lacked poise. And she was ashamed on their behalf. Sometimes she wondered if she wasn't an orphan that they had adopted.

'I tell you, she's worrying me. She's very thin,' said Denis.

'So? She's a dancer,' replied Clémence.

'Not all dancers are as thin as that.'

'She's thirteen. It's normal at that age.'

Reassured by this argument, Denis was able to get to sleep. The parental capacity for wilful blindness is immense. By beginning with a precise observation – the frequent occurrence of thinness among adolescents – they managed to blot out their individual circumstances. Their daughter was slender by nature, certainly: none the less, her present thinness wasn't natural.

The holiday came and went. Plectrude went back to school, to her very great relief.

'Sometimes I feel as though I've lost a child,' said Denis.

'You're selfish,' protested Clémence. 'She's happy.'

She was wrong on both counts. First of all, the little girl was not happy. Secondly, her husband's selfishness was as nothing compared to her own: she would so have liked to be a ballerina and, thanks to Plectrude, she had satisfied that ambition vicariously. It little mattered if she sacrificed the health of her child to that ideal. If anyone had said that to her, she would have opened her eyes wide and exclaimed, 'All I want is for my daughter to be happy!'

And for her part her observation would have been an honest one. Parents don't know what lies concealed behind their own sincerity.

WHAT PLECTRUDE WAS GOING THROUGH at the école des rats was not the thing called happiness: that requires a minimum sense of security. The little girl did not have the merest hint of that, and she was right not to: at her stage of life she was no longer playing with her health, she was gambling on it now. She knew that.

What Plectrude was going through at the école des rats was called intoxication: that form of ecstasy that is fed on a massive dose of oblivion. Forgetting privations, physical suffering, danger, fear. Through such voluntary amnesia she was able to throw herself into dancing, and know the mad illusion of it, the trance of flight.

She was becoming one of the school's best pupils. Certainly, she was not the thinnest of them, but she was without contest the most graceful: she possessed that marvellous ease of movement that is the most supreme injustice of nature, because grace is given or withheld at birth, and no subsequent effort can compensate for its absence.

And then there was the fact, which did her no harm at

all, that she was the prettiest of them all. Even at five and a half stone, she didn't look like those corpses whose thinness the teachers praised: she had her dancer's eyes which lit up her face with their fantastic beauty. And the teachers knew, without mentioning it to their pupils, that prettiness is enormously important in the choice of star dancers; in this respect, Plectrude was by some way the most fortunate.

It was her health that worried her in secret. She didn't talk to anyone about it, but at night her legs hurt so much that she had to stop herself from shouting. Although she had not the slightest notion about medicine, she suspected the reason: she had cut even the slightest trace of dairy products out of her diet. She had actually noticed that a few spoonfuls of low-fat yoghurt were enough to make her feel 'bloated' (and what she meant by 'bloated' is hard for the rest of us to grasp).

Indeed, low-fat yoghurt was the only form of lactose permitted in the school. Doing without it meant eliminating any intake of calcium, which was supposed to cement adolescence. Mad as the adults at the school might have been, none of them recommended doing without yoghurt, and even the most emaciated of them consumed it. Plectrude banned it from her diet.

Very quickly, this deficiency led to atrocious pains in her legs whenever she had to stay motionless for a few hours, as she did at night. To get rid of the pain she had to get up and move about. But the moment her legs started moving again she suffered agonies worthy of a torture chamber: Plectrude had to bite on a rag to keep from screaming. Each time, she felt as though the bones in her calves and thighs were about to snap.

She understood that decalcification was the cause of her torment. But she couldn't bring herself to start eating that wretched yoghurt again. Without knowing it, she was falling victim to the internal machinery of anorexia, which considers each fresh privation impossible to reverse except at the cost of an unendurable sense of guilt.

She lost another four and a half pounds, which confirmed her conviction that low-fat yoghurt was 'heavy'. During the Easter holidays, her father told her she had turned into a skeleton and that it was horrible to see, but her mother immediately talked over Denis and went into raptures about her daughter's beauty. Clémence was the only member of the family that Plectrude was still happy to see: 'At least she understands me.' Her sisters and even Roselyne looked upon her as a stranger. She was no longer part of their group: they didn't feel anything in common with that assemblage of bones.

Since dropping below five stone three, the dancer had even fewer emotions than before. So the family's exclusion of her caused her no pain.

Plectrude admired her life: she felt as though she was the sole heroine in a battle against gravity. She waged war upon it with the twin weapons of fasting and dance.

The Holy Grail was flight and, of all the knights, Plectrude was the most likely to attain it. What mattered her nocturnal pains in the face of the immensity of her quest?

The months and years passed. The dancer was integrated within her school like a Carmelite within her order. There could be no salvation outside of the establishment.

She was the rising star. She was discussed at the highest levels: she knew that.

She reached the age of fifteen. She still measured five foot two, which meant that she hadn't grown so much as an inch since entering the école des rats. Her weight: five stone exactly.

It sometimes seemed to her that she had had no life before this. She hoped that her existence would never change. Other people's admiration, whether real or imagined, was enough of an emotional relationship for her.

She knew too that her mother loved her to distraction. Although she didn't show it, the awareness of that love served as her spinal column. One day, she mentioned the leg problem to Clémence; her mother said only, 'How brave you are!'

Plectrude savoured the compliment. But within herself, she had a sense that her mother should have said something very different. She didn't know what.

The inevitable happened. One November morning, when Plectrude had just got out of bed, biting her rag so as not to howl with pain, she collapsed: she heard a cracking noise in her thigh.

She couldn't move. She called for help. She was put in hospital.

A doctor who hadn't seen her before looked at her X-rays.

'How old is this woman?'

'Fifteen.'

'What? She's got the bones of a menopausal sixty-year-old!'

They asked her some questions. She told them straight out: she hadn't had any dairy products for two years – at the age when the body craves them.

'Are you anorexic?'

'No, for heaven's sake!' she protested, in good faith.

'Do you think it's normal to weigh four and a half stone at your age?'

'Five!' she protested.

'What difference do you think that makes?'

She resorted to Clémence's arguments: 'I'm a ballerina. It's better not to have curves in my job.'

'I didn't know they'd started recruiting dancers from the concentration camps.'

'You're mad! You're insulting my school!'

'So what do you think about an establishment where an adolescent is allowed to self-destruct? I'm going to call the police,' said the fearless doctor.

Plectrude instinctively leapt to the defence of her order.

'No! It's my fault! I stopped eating it in secret! No one knew.'

'No one wanted to know. The result is that you've broken your tibia just by falling on the ground. If you were normal, a month in plaster would be enough. In your condition, I don't know how many months you're going to have to keep the plaster on. Not to mention the rehabilitation you'll have to go through afterwards.'

'But does that mean I won't be able to dance for a long time?'

'My dear girl, you'll never be able to dance again.'

Plectrude's heart stopped beating. She sank into a sort of coma.

She emerged from it a number of days later. Once she had passed that exquisite moment when the memory is blank, she remembered the sentence passed on her. A pleasant nurse confirmed her punishment:

'Your bones are seriously weakened, especially in your legs. Even when your tibia is mended, you won't be able to start dancing again. The slightest jump, the slightest impact could bruise you. It will take years of extra dairy products to bring your calcium levels back up to normal.'

Telling Plectrude that she wouldn't be dancing again was like telling Napoleon he wouldn't have an army again: it was to deprive her not only of her vocation, but of her destiny.

She couldn't believe it. She fired questions at every doctor she could think of: not one gave her the faintest glimmer of hope. They are to be congratulated: if even one of them had given her a hundredth of a chance of recovery, she would have clung to it, with fatal consequences.

After a few days, Plectrude was surprised that Clémence hadn't come to her bedside. She asked to make a phone call. Her father told her that when the terrible news had come, her mother had fallen seriously ill:

'She's running a fever, she's delirious. She thinks she's you. She says, "I'm only fifteen, my dream can't be over yet, I'm going to be a dancer, I can't be anything but a dancer!"'

The idea of Clémence in pain was the final straw for Plectrude. In her hospital bed, she studied the drip that was feeding her: she was truly convinced that it was injecting her with unhappiness in the guise of food.

While she was forbidden to make the slightest movement, Plectrude remained in hospital. Her father sometimes came to visit her. She asked why Clémence didn't come with him.

'Your mother's still too ill,' he replied.

That went on for several months. No one else came to see her, no one from the école des rats, or from her family, or from her former school: it was as though Plectrude no longer belonged to any world.

She spent her days doing absolutely nothing. She didn't want to read anything, either books or newspapers. She refused to watch television. She was diagnosed as suffering from deep depression.

She couldn't swallow anything. A good thing she had her drip-feed. But it disgusted her: it was what connected her with life, in spite of herself.

When springtime came, she was taken to see her parents. Her heart pounded at the idea of seeing her mother again: her wish was refused. The young girl protested: 'That's not possible! Is she dead, or what?'

'No, she's alive, but she doesn't want you to see her in this state.'

It was more than Plectrude could bear. She waited until her sisters were at school and her father had gone out before she left her bed: by now she was able to move around on crutches.

She tottered as far as her parents' bedroom, where Clémence was sleeping. When she saw her, the girl thought she was dead: she had a grey complexion, and seemed even thinner than her daughter. She collapsed at her side, weeping, 'Mama! Mama!'

The sleeping woman woke up and said, 'You're not allowed in here.'

'But I had to see you. And anyway I've done it now, and it's better that way: I'd rather know how you are. As long as you're alive, nothing else matters. You're going to start eating, you'll get better: we're both going to get better, Mama.'

She noticed that her mother was still cold, and that she wasn't hugging her.

'Hold me in your arms, I so need you to!'

Clémence remained inert.

'Poor Mama, you're too weak even for that.'

She stood up and looked at her. How she had changed! There was no longer any warmth in her mother's eyes. Something had died in her: Plectrude didn't want to understand it.

She said to herself: 'Mama thinks she's me. She's stopped eating because I stopped eating. If I eat, she will eat. If I get better, she will get better.'

The girl dragged herself as far as the kitchen and picked up a bar of chocolate. Then she came back to Clémence's bedroom and sat down on the bed, near her.

'Look, Mama, I'm eating.'

The chocolate was a shock to her mouth, which was no longer used to food, let alone such a rich confection. Plectrude forced herself not to reveal her illness.

'It's milk chocolate, Mama, it's full of calcium. It's good for me.'

So that was what eating was? Her innards shuddered, her stomach revolted. Plectrude felt she was about to keel over, but she didn't faint: she vomited, on her knees.

Humiliated, desolate, she remained motionless, contemplating her work.

It was then that her mother said dryly: 'You disgust me.'

The girl looked at the glacial eye of the woman who had just delivered such a judgement upon her. She didn't want to believe what she had heard and seen. She fled as quickly as her crutches allowed.

Plectrude fell on her bed and sobbed her heart out. She went to sleep.

When she woke up, she became aware of an unlikely phenomenon: she was hungry.

She asked Béatrice, who had come back in the meantime, to bring her a tray.

'Victory!' applauded her sister, who soon brought her bread, some cheese, stewed fruit, ham and chocolate.

The girl refused the chocolate, which reminded her too clearly of her recent vomiting; in compensation, she devoured the rest.

Béatrice exulted.

Plectrude's appetite had returned. This was not bulimia, but healthy, greedy hunger. She ate three copious meals a day, feeling particularly attracted to cheese, as though her body were informing her about its most urgent needs. Her father and her sisters were delighted.

On this diet, Plectrude quickly put on weight. She reattained her six and a half stone and her beautiful face. Everything was for the best. She even managed not to feel guilty, which, for a former anorexic, is really quite extraordinary.

As she had predicted, her recovery meant her mother's recovery as well. Her mother finally left her room and saw her daughter again, not having even so much as glimpsed her since the day when she had vomited. She looked at her with consternation, and cried, 'You've got fatter!'

'Yes, Mama,' stammered the girl.

'What possessed you? You were so pretty before!'

'Don't you think I'm pretty like this?'

'No, you're fat.'

'But Mama! I weigh six and a half stone!'

'Exactly: you've put on a stone and a half.'

'I had to!'

'That's what you say to ease your conscience. It was calcium you needed, not weight. Do you think you look like a dancer now?'

'But Mama, I can't dance any more. I'm not a dancer any

more. Do you know how much pain I'm in? Don't twist the knife in the wound!'

'If you were in pain, you wouldn't be so hungry.'

The worst thing was the hard voice with which the woman delivered her verdict.

'Why do you talk like that? Am I not your daughter?'

'You've never been my daughter.'

CLÉMENCE TOLD HER EVERYTHING: Lucette, Fabien, Fabien's murder at the hands of Lucette, her birth in prison, Lucette's suicide.

'What are you telling me?' moaned Plectrude.

'Ask your father – or rather, your uncle – if you don't believe me.'

Once her initial disbelief had passed, the girl managed to say, 'Why are you telling me this today?'

'I was going to have to tell you some day, wasn't I?'

'Of course. But why in such a cruel way? You've always been a wonderful mother. Now you're talking to me as though I had never been your daughter.'

'Because you've betrayed me. You know how much I dreamt of you being a dancer.'

'I had an accident! It's not my fault.'

'Yes, it is your fault! If you hadn't stupidly decalcified yourself!'

'I talked to you about the pains in my legs!'

'That's not true!'

'Yes it is, I talked to you about it! You even congratulated me on my courage.'

'You're lying!'

'I don't lie! Do you think it's normal for a mother to congratulate her daughter on having pains in her legs? It was a cry for help, and you didn't even hear it.'

'That's right, say it's my fault.'

Clémence's bad faith left Plectrude speechless.

Her world collapsed: she had no destiny, no parents, she had nothing now.

Denis was nice but weak. Clémence told him to stop congratulating Plectrude for regaining her appetite: 'Don't encourage her to get fat, for heaven's sake!'

'She's not fat,' he bleated. 'A bit plump, perhaps.'

That phrase, 'a bit plump', told the girl that she had lost an ally.

Telling a fifteen-year-old girl that she's fat, or even 'a bit plump', when she weighs six and a half stone, is the same as telling her she mustn't grow up.

Faced with a disaster on that scale, a girl has only two choices: falling back into anorexia, or bulimia. Miraculously, Plectrude didn't succumb to either. She kept her appetite. She had a hunger that any doctor would have considered healthy, and which Clémence declared to be 'monstrous'.

In fact, it was her health that told Plectrude to be hungry: she had years of adolescence to catch up on. Thanks to her frenetic consumption of cheese she grew an inch and a half.

None the less, five foot three and a half was better than five foot two as a height for an adult.

When she was sixteen, she had her first period. She told Clémence as though it was a marvellous piece of news. Clémence shrugged her shoulders contemptuously.

'Aren't you pleased that I'm finally normal?'

'How much do you weigh?'

'Eight stone.'

'That's what I thought. You're obese.'

'Eight stone and a height of five foot three and a half, do you think that's obese?'

'Look the truth in the face: you're enormous.'

Plectrude, who had regained the full use of her legs, went and threw herself on her bed. She didn't cry: she felt a pang of hatred that lasted for hours. She struck her pillow with her fist and, inside her skull, a voice howled, 'She wants to kill me! My mother wants me dead!'

She had never stopped thinking of Clémence as her mother: it didn't matter whether she had come out of her belly or not. She was her mother because she was the one who had really given her life – and now it was she who wanted to take it away.

In her place, many adolescents would have committed suicide. The survival instinct must have been unbelievably deep-rooted in Plectrude because she finally got up, saying in a loud, calm voice: 'I won't let myself be killed, Mama.'

She took herself in hand again, insofar as that was possible for a sixteen-year-old girl who had lost everything. Since her mother had gone mad, she would be an adult in her place.

She signed up for drama classes. She made a great impression. Her first name contributed to that. Being called Plectrude was a twin-edged blade: either you were ugly and the name underlined your ugliness, or you were beautiful and the strange sonority of Plectrude increased your beauty a hundredfold.

That was her case. People were already struck when they saw that girl with the wonderful eyes and the dancer's gait entering a room. When they discovered her first name, they looked at her even more closely, and admired her sublime hair, her tragic expression, her perfect mouth, her ideal complexion.

Her teacher told her she had 'a physique' (she thought it was a strange expression: didn't everyone have a physique?) and advised her to start going to castings.

That was how she came to be selected to play the part of the adolescent Geraldine Chaplin in a television film; when she saw her, the actress exclaimed, 'I wasn't as beautiful as that at her age!' But it couldn't be denied that there was a certain similarity between the two faces, both extremely thin.

That kind of performance brought the girl a small income, but unfortunately not enough to let her get away from her mother, which had been her intention. In the evenings she got back to the apartment as late as possible, so as not to bump into Clémence. But she wasn't always able to avoid her, and she found herself being welcomed with, 'Hey! Here comes the fat girl!'

That was if she was lucky. The worst one was, 'Evening, Blubber!'

One might find it hard to imagine how hurtful such comments were; that would be to ignore the air of disgust with which they were delivered.

One day, Plectrude dared to reply that Béatrice, who weighed a stone more than she did, never received such disobliging remarks. To which her mother replied, 'That's irrelevant, as you know very well.'

She wasn't bold enough to say no, she didn't 'know very well'. All she understood was that her sister was allowed to be normal, and she was not.

One evening, when Plectrude had been unable to find an excuse not to have dinner with her family, and when Clémence assumed a scandalized expression every time she swallowed a mouthful, she finally protested, 'Mama, stop looking at me like that! Have you never seen anyone eating before?'

'It's for your own good, my darling. I'm worried about your bulimia.'

'Bulimia!'

Plectrude stared at her father, then at her sisters, before saying, 'You're too cowardly to defend me!'

Her father stammered, 'I'm not bothered if you've got a good appetite.'

'Coward!' cried the girl. 'I eat less than you do.'

Nicole shrugged her shoulders.

'I don't give a damn about all your crap.'

'I might have expected that from you,' screeched the adolescent.

Béatrice took a deep breath and then said, 'Right, Mama, I'd like you to leave my sister in peace, OK?'

'Thanks,' said the girl.

It was at that moment that Clémence smiled and proclaimed, 'She's not your sister, Béatrice!'

'What are you on about?'

'Do you think this is quite the moment?' murmured Denis.

Clémence got up and went to get a photograph, which she threw on the table.

'This is Lucette, my sister, Plectrude's real mother.'

As she told Nicole and Béatrice the story, the girl grabbed the photograph and looked avidly at the dead woman's pretty face.

The sisters were flabbergasted.

'I look like her,' said Plectrude.

She reflected that her mother had committed suicide at the age of nineteen, and that that would be her fate, too. 'I'm sixteen. Another three years to live, and a child to bring into the world.'

From that moment onwards Plectrude looked at the many boys who buzzed around her with different, older eyes. She couldn't stare at them without thinking, 'Would I like to have his baby?'

More often than not, the answer deep within herself was

no. The idea of having a child with one young dandy or another seemed quite unthinkable to her.

In her drama classes, the teacher decided that Plectrude and one of her fellow students would play a scene from *The Bald Prima Donna*. The girl was so profoundly intrigued by the text that she got hold of the complete works of Ionesco. It was a revelation: she suddenly discovered that fever that makes you go on reading for whole nights at a time.

She had often tried to read, but the books fell from her hands. Perhaps for every human being there is, within the universe of the written word, a work that will turn that person into a reader, if destiny permits. What Plato says about the loving half, that other part who is circling around somewhere and must be found if one is not to remain incomplete until one's dying day, holds even more true where books are concerned.

'Ionesco is the author destined for me,' the girl thought. She drew considerable happiness from this, the intoxication that can come only from discovering a book that you love.

In some people, that first literary passion leads to a love of reading; this was not the case with our heroine, who only opened other books to confirm how boring she thought they were. She decided she would read no other author, and prided herself on her loyalty.

One evening when she was watching television, Plectrude learned of the existence of the French chanteuse Catherine Ringer. She heard her singing, and felt a mixture of infatuation and bitterness: infatuation because she thought she was amazing; bitterness because that sort of singing was exactly what she would have liked to do herself, but she had neither the ability, nor the funds, nor the slightest notion of how to go about it.

If she had been the kind of girl who had a different ambition every week, it wouldn't have mattered so much. Unfortunately, that was not the case. At the age of seventeen, Plectrude wasn't an enthusiast. She couldn't get terribly worked up about her drama classes. She would have sold her soul to take up dancing again, but the doctors, while they had observed a distinct progress in her recalcification, were unanimous in forbidding her to return to her old vocation.

The reason the discovery of Catherine Ringer was such a shock to the teenager was that for the first time it gave her a dream that had nothing at all to do with dancing.

She consoled herself with the thought that she was going to die in two years anyway, and that in the meantime she had to bring a child into the world. 'I haven't got time to be a singer,' she thought to herself.

In her drama classes, Plectrude had to act out a passage from Ionesco's *The Lesson*. For an actor, getting one of the main roles in a work by your favourite playwright is at once Byzantium and Cythera, Rome and the Vatican.

It would not be true to say that she *became* the young pupil in the play. She had always been that part, a girl so enthusiastic about her chosen apprenticeships that she has managed to pervert and destroy them all – encouraged and anticipated in that, of course, by her teacher, that great chewer-up of knowledge and students.

She was the pupil with such a sense of the sacred that it contaminated the other part: the actor who was to play the part of the teacher was automatically chosen by Plectrude.

During a rehearsal, in response to a line miraculous in its truthfulness ('Philology leads to crime'), she told him he would be the father of her child. He thought this was a linguistic device worthy of *The Bald Prima Donna*, and agreed. That night, she took him at his word.

A month later, Plectrude knew that she was pregnant. A warning to those, if they exist, who still see Ionesco only as a comic writer.

PLECTRUDE WAS THE SAME AGE as her mother had been when she gave birth: nineteen. The baby was called Simon. He was beautiful and healthy.

The adolescent felt a fabulous surge of love when she saw him. She hadn't expected to possess maternal fibre to such an extent, and she was sorry about it: 'Suicide's not going to be easy.'

But she was determined to take things to their conclusion: 'I've already made concessions to fate by deciding not to kill Simon's father. But I'm not going to get myself out of it.'

She rocked the child, murmuring, 'I love you, Simon, I love you. I'll die because die I must. If I could choose, I would stay near you. But I must die: it's an order, I can feel it.'

A week later, she said to herself: 'It's now or never. If I go on living, I'm going to get too attached to Simon. The longer I wait, the harder it's going to be.'

She didn't write a letter, for the noble reason that she didn't like writing. At any rate, what she was about to do seemed legible enough without further explanation.

Lacking the courage for the deed, she decided to put on her finest clothes: she had already noticed that elegance fired the spirits.

Two years previously, at a flea-market, she had found a dress that had once belonged to some phantasmagorical grand-duchess, midnight blue with old lace, so sumptuous that it couldn't be worn.

'If I don't wear it today, I'll never wear it,' she said to herself, before bursting out laughing as she realized how profoundly true her reflection was.

Pregnancy had left her a little thinner, and she floated in her dress: she made the best of it. She let down her magnificent hair, which fell to her bottom. Once she had made herself up to look like a tragic fairy she was pleased, and told herself she could now kill herself without blushing.

Plectrude kissed Simon. The moment she left her apartment she wondered how she was going to do it: would she throw herself under a train, under a car, or into the Seine? She hadn't even asked herself the question: 'I'll just see,' she concluded. 'If you worried about that sort of detail you'd never do anything.'

She walked as far as the station. She hadn't the courage to throw herself under the wheels of the RER train. 'Where dying's concerned, it would be best to do it in Paris, and in the least awful way,' she said to herself, with a certain sense of what was right and proper. So she boarded the train. Never in the history of the suburban line could anyone remember ever having seen a passenger looking so wonderful, all the more so because she was grinning from ear to ear: the prospect of suicide put her in excellent humour.

She went into the centre of the city and walked along the Seine, in search of the bridge best suited to her undertaking. As she couldn't make her mind up between the Pont Alexandre III, the Pont des Arts and the Pont-Neuf, she walked around for a long time, constantly coming and going to reconsider their respective merits.

In the end the Pont Alexandre III failed by virtue of excessive magnificence, and the Pont des Arts was ruled out for an excess of intimacy. She had chosen the Pont-Neuf both because it was old and because it had semi-circular platforms, ideally suited for last-minute changes of mind.

Men and women turned their heads at the sight of this beautiful woman, too absorbed in her project to notice. Not since her childhood had she felt so euphoric.

She sat down on the edge of the bridge, her feet dangling in the void. Many people sat like this, and it didn't attract anyone's attention. She looked around her. A grey sky hung over Notre Dame, the water of the Seine trembled in the wind. Suddenly Plectrude was struck by the great age of the world: how quickly her nineteen years would be swallowed up in the centuries of Paris!

She felt dizzy, and her exaltation subsided: all that grandeur of durable things, all that eternity that she wouldn't be a part of! Into the world she had brought a child who wouldn't remember her. Apart from that, nothing. The only person she had loved was her mother: in killing herself, she would be obeying the mother she no longer loved. 'That's not true: there's Simon as well. I love him. But given how damaging a mother's love is, it would be better for me to spare him that.'

Beneath her feet, the river's great void beckoned.

'Why did I have to wait for this moment to feel what I have been lacking? My life is racked with hunger and thirst, nothing has ever happened to me to feed and water my life, my heart has dried up, my head is starving, I have a gaping hole where my soul should be, is this the state in which I must die?'

The void roared around her. The question crushed her, she was tempted to escape it by letting her feet become heavier than her brain.

At that very moment, a voice yelled in the distance: 'Plectrude!'

'Is that a voice from among the living or the dead?' she wondered.

She leaned towards the water, as though she might see someone in it.

The shout doubled in intensity: 'Plectrude!'

It was a man's voice.

She turned towards the place where the shout was coming from.

THAT DAY, MATHIEU SALADIN had felt some obscure need to leave his native seventeenth arrondissement to walk along the Seine.

He was enjoying the mild, grey day, when he saw an apparition coming in the opposite direction on the pavement: a girl of dazzling beauty dressed as though for a fancy-dress ball.

He had stopped to watch her pass. She hadn't seen him. She didn't see anyone, with her big, astounding eyes. It was at that moment that he recognized her. He had smiled with joy: 'I've found her! She seems to be just as mad as before. This time I'm not going to let her go.'

He had given himself up to that pleasure that comes from secretly following someone you know, observing their behaviour, interpreting their actions.

When she had turned into the Pont-Neuf, even knowing its reputation as a bridge for suicides, he hadn't been worried: he had seen a happy expression on her face, she didn't look desperate. He had rested his elbows on the balustrade along the Seine and leaned forward to see his former classmate.

Gradually it had occurred to him that Plectrude was behaving very oddly. Her very exaltation had struck him as suspect; when he had the distinct impression that she was going to throw herself in the river, he yelled her name and ran towards her.

She recognized him immediately.

They had the shortest amorous prelude in history.

'Are you with anybody?' asked Mathieu, not wasting a second.

'Single, with a baby,' she replied, just as crisply.

'Perfect. Want me?'

'Yes.'

He gripped Plectrude's hips and turned them through one hundred and eighty degrees so that her feet weren't in the void. They French-kissed for a moment to seal what had been said.

'You weren't going to kill yourself, by any chance?'

'No,' she replied out of modesty.

He locked lips with her again. She thought: 'A minute ago I was about to throw myself into the void, and now I'm in the arms of the love of my life, a man I haven't seen for seven years, whom I thought I'd never see again. I'm deciding to put off my death to some later date.'

Plectrude discovered a surprising thing: you could be happy once you'd reached adulthood.

'I'm going to show you where I live,' he said, taking her there.

'You don't waste your time!'

'I've wasted seven years. That's quite enough.'

If Mathieu Saladin had had any notion of the earful that his confession was about to bring him, he would have kept his trap shut. Time after time Plectrude yelled at him, 'And to think you made me wait seven years! And to think you made me suffer!'

To which Mathieu protested, 'You left me too! Why didn't you tell me you loved me when we were twelve?'

'The boy's supposed to do that,' Plectrude retorted bossily.

One day when Plectrude was launching off on the familiar refrain, '. . . and to think you made me wait seven years!' Mathieu broke in with a revelation.

'You're not the only one who's been in hospital. Between the ages of twelve and eighteen I was hospitalized six times.'

'So you've found yourself a new excuse, have you? And for what trivial ailment, pray, were you being treated?'

'To be more precise, perhaps you ought to know that between the ages of one and eighteen I was hospitalized eighteen times.'

She frowned.

'It's a long story,' he began.

At the age of one, Mathieu Saladin had died.

Baby Mathieu Saladin was crawling through his parents' sitting room, exploring the exciting universe of the feet of armchairs and the undersides of tables. Plugged into an electrical socket there was an extension lead that wasn't connected to anything else. The baby took an interest in this wire, which ended in a captivating plastic bulb. He put it in his mouth and salivated. He received a shock that killed him.

Mathieu's father refused to accept his death-sentence by electrocution. During the hour that followed, he drove the baby to the best doctor on the planet. No one knew what happened, but he brought the little body back to life.

He still had to be given a mouth. Mathieu Saladin no longer had anything that might have merited the name: no lips, no palate. The doctor sent him to the best surgeon in the universe, who took a little bit of cartilage here, a bit of skin there, and, at the end of his painstaking patchwork, reconstructed, if not a mouth, at least the structure of one.

'That's all I can do for now,' he concluded. 'Come back in a year's time.'

Every year he performed another operation on Mathieu Saladin, each time adding something new. Then he finished with the two sentences that had by now become a ritual. It was the subject of jokes throughout the miracle boy's childhood and adolescence.

'And if you're very good, next year we'll give you an uvula' (or a velar membrane, a palatal curve, a gingivoplasty, etc.).

Plectrude listened to him, in the realms of ecstasy.

'That's why you've got that sublime scar on your moustache?'

'Sublime?'

'There's nothing more beautiful!'

They were really destined for each other, those two creatures. In the course of the first year of their lives each of them, in such different ways, had come far too close to death.

The many fairies – too many – who had encumbered the girl with ordeals to match the graces they had bestowed upon her, then sent her the worst of the plagues of Egypt: a plague from Belgium.

A few years had passed. Experiencing perfect love with Mathieu Saladin, a musician by trade, had given Plectrude the courage to become a singer, under a pseudonym which was the name of a French dictionary, and which was thus ideally suited to the encyclopaedic dimensions of the suffering she had known: Robert.

In most cases the greatest misfortunes assume the face of friendship: Plectrude met Amélie Nothomb and saw in her the friend, the sister that she so needed.

Plectrude told her about her life. Amélie listened with alarm to this tale of tragic destiny. She asked her if so many attempts to murder her hadn't given her the desire to kill, by that law that turns victims into the best of executioners.

'Your father was murdered by your mother when she was carrying you, in the eighth month of her pregnancy. We're sure that you were awake because you had the hiccups. So you're a witness!'

'But I didn't see anything!'

'You must have been aware of something. You're a witness of a very special kind: a witness *in utero*. They say that in their mothers' bellies babies hear music and know when their parents are making love. Your mother emptied the magazine into your father, in a state of extreme violence: you must have felt it, one way or another.'

'Where are we going with this, exactly?'

'You're filled to the brim with that murder. Let's not even talk about the metaphorical attempted murders that have been imposed upon you, and which you've subsequently imposed upon yourself. How could you have helped becoming a murderess?'

Plectrude, who would never have thought of that, could think of nothing else from that point onwards. And as a form of justice does exist, she satisfied her murderous desire upon the very person who had suggested it. She took the rifle that never left her side, and which came in useful when she went to see her producers, and fired it straight at Amélie's temple.

'It's the only way I've managed to get her to shut up,' she told her husband, curtly.

Plectrude and Mathieu, both of whom had often crossed the river of Hell, looked at the corpse with a tear in the corner of their eyes. Yet more connivance between such a touching couple.

From that point onwards, one syllable aside, their life became an Ionesco play: *Amélie, or How to Get Rid of It*. It was a very troublesome cadaver.

Murder has this in common with the sexual act: it is often followed by the same question – what should we do with the body? In the case of sex, you can simply part company. With murder, things aren't so easy. It's partly for that reason that it's a much stronger bond between people.

As things stand, Plectrude and Mathieu still haven't come up with a solution.